Styrofoam Throne

Styrofoam Throne

---

by David Bone

Jawbreaker Books

Cover art by Nick Lakiotes

ISBN 978-0-9894152-0-0

Jawbreaker Books

www.DavidBoneBooks.com

To Stephanie

1

It was the last day of high school before the summer of 1984. A total jack-off day, for sure. I slouched in the back of class and hid behind my shaggy, black hair. My legs were out in the aisles because they wouldn't fit under the desk. But really, nothing about me fit in at school. Surrounded by red-blooded, all-American assholes, I was a horror-obsessed loner. Everyone was buzzing with countdown fever. Their smiles and conspiratorial camaraderie took over the normally somber room. The only thing we did was get our tests back from the day before. The teacher handed each one back with a cookie and a look that projected your grade. I didn't have anyone to talk to, so I ate mine as slowly as possible.

Looking for something else to pay attention to, I zeroed in on a kid wearing a Castle Dunes T-shirt. It was a seasonal haunted attraction anchored to our town's pier. The commercials and brochures claimed it to be "the largest haunted walk-through attraction in America!" Its five stories dominated the coastline and represented the town's signature landmark. And my obsession.

"I was the first one in yesterday!" the kid with the T-shirt said.

"Whoa, so what's it like this year?" another asked.

"It's fucking insane!"

"Ricky! Watch your mouth, young man," the teacher said, looking up from her romance novel.

"Anyways, I can't believe I'm alive!"

Our town, Dunes, was about halfway up the California coast. Going to the Castle was really the only thing to do during the summer.

I needed an excuse to get closer to the conversation without crossing the social boundary. I picked up an already sharpened pencil, broke the tip, and walked to the wall-mounted sharpener in front.

"I saw the most fucked-up—sorry, Ms. K—like, satanic slaughter room where there was this evil dude with a pentagram branded on his chest, and he was just stabbing the shit out of this hot chick with green hair." The kid continued on in a whisper. "She was wearing, like, this white sacrificial robe, but it was all bloody by her tits, so you could totally see nipples."

"Oh shit! That one in the commercial?" one of them asked.

"No, bigger tits. She's new, I think."

The impressed group nodded in silence at this info. But I couldn't hold back, I had a million questions to ask. I had never been inside.

"Did… did you see Dracula?" I asked.

The group turned their heads in synchronicity and shot me a death stare. I cranked my pencil with renewed purpose. Of course I knew it wasn't *the* Dracula, but it was *a* Dracula and that was plenty cool.

"What're you doing?" the kid said, motioning to my shrinking pencil. "Making a to-scale model of your dick?"

"Ricky!" The teacher sighed and left the room with her coffee cup.

As the door shut, the group erupted in laughter. Everyone was into Castle Dunes but I was really, really into Castle Dunes. Generally, my enthusiasm for things I liked was unparalleled by others and left me feeling alone. In high school, common interests were only a bond if one wasn't obsessively interested. Unable to relate to simple amusement, I'd slipped up and revealed that something was actually important to me.

"Did, did I see Dracula?! Donovan, you look like you already work there, you fuckin' weirdo," Ricky said.

Now the entire class was laughing as I cranked away. If the tone of his remark had been more complimentary, I couldn't think of higher praise. But it was definitely not praise.

"Prince of Dorkness!" another student said as the laughs kept coming.

If it was anyone but me, I would have been included in the conversation and had my question answered with "Yeah, bro!" But almost everyone hated me after what happened at the freshman talent show.

It was all stupid, normal stuff like football players dressing up like cheerleaders and vice versa. My "talent" ended up being a little too high and wide for the audience though. I dressed up like a magician and pulled a rabbit out of my hat. The crowd couldn't even pretend to be patient. They had their groans and shouts of "Next!" ready when they first saw me walk out. But that wasn't the trick. Suddenly, the rabbit turned on me and started attacking my throat. To the audience's horror, I ripped it apart in defense, sending blood and fur flying everywhere. The crowd screamed bloody murder while the principal hurried on stage to escort me off. No one let me finish the trick. If they had, I could have revealed that the rabbit was fake and that it was a trick within a trick. No one believed me. So from then on, I was the freak who exhibited early serial killer behavior on stage.

But in class, I stuck to the loop of furious sharpening until the metal band holding the eraser hit the sharpener inside with a ripping clank. I left the remains stuck inside and walked back to my desk. Various classmates were still turning around and directing their sputtering chuckles at me. I slouched in my desk as much as possible before sliding under it. Everyone went back to detailing their plans of sun-drenched anarchy. They couldn't wait to be together this summer. I couldn't wait to be alone.

I think the girls hated me more than the guys. Of course I wanted to hook up with chicks at school but it was a one-sided interest. I never had the chance to act on any of my feelings, or even the chance to shyly not act on them. One time, a girl at school who wasn't so much a friend but a person who took pity on me told me that she knew of a "couple girls" who would like me "if you'd only change the way you look." I'd rather they just hate me. And how come they'd like me if they wanted me to change? It only made me want to hide behind my horror magazines at lunch even more.

I did have one friend, Egon. Maybe we were more like lonely acquaintances. But he was going away all summer to space camp. He was fascinated not by space itself but by the machinery it took to get there. We would sit around at lunch or wander the forests after school and patiently listen to each other's monologues about shit we liked, then pass the mic. We respected each other's weird obsessions even if we didn't share them. But I wouldn't even have that this summer.

I took the long way home so I could cut through Odd Fellows Cemetery. Around town, it was the closest thing to a park that didn't have barbecues and basketball courts. No one was ever in it except for the occasional caretaker and me. It felt like I owned the biggest plot of land in town for free and just had to share it with some very quiet, unobtrusive tenants. It was cool to loiter around, imagining creepy things unfolding, but no amount of real corpses beneath my feet could satisfy my longing for fake ones. The Odd Fellows seemed too content to bother spooking their remains. I wanted balls-to-the-Castle-walls horror. No one thought the cemetery was fun, not even me, but I worked with what I had. While other kids were hitting the pavement in convoys of bikes and skateboards, I pondered the dark side of the tomb.

I once saw people fucking in the graveyard and hung around to watch them. My only experience with sex was a couple weathered porno mags I found under the bridge, so I chalked my voyeurism up to educational observation. But I got caught. The girl saw me and sent the guy running after me while he tried pulling up his pants. I got away but they both went to Dunes High and told everyone I jacked off in the cemetery. I wasn't jacking off. Not like I didn't memorize the scene for later. But between that and the talent show, I was ruined.

My mom, Janice, and I lived in a one-story, two-bedroom house. Featuring tan stucco and brown trim, it was no Castle. Our lawn never looked green, but it wasn't all dirt either. Just dry, pale grass that wouldn't give up. Her orange VW Bug was parked in the driveway, which was strange because she normally waitressed Fridays at The Roost, the local diner.

I walked in the door and saw Janice sitting in her living room chair, waiting. Her long brown hair was permanently and tightly pulled back, showing off tired eyes and the beginning of a sagging face that had long ago lost its ability to smile off the clock. Hers used to be a different story. She had once been a glamorous magician's assistant with big dreams, until she got knocked up. The magician kept her on until she couldn't fit in the trap door any longer. That's when he left her in the middle of the night, pulling one last disappearing act in the Koko Motel parking lot. That's the only story she ever told me about my father.

"Hey," I said.

"Where have you been? School got out over two hours ago," Janice said. I felt like I had walked into the middle of an argument.

"The cemetery."

Janice rolled her eyes.

"How was school?"

"Glad it's over."

"Well, don't think you're on Easy Street, mister."

"I think Easy Street is on the other side of town."

"Real funny. You're not gonna get away with staring at your shoes all summer long. You're sixteen, so that means you can work at The Roost now."

"What?!" I said. I couldn't believe it and like most cornered guys, my only defense was "What?!"

"Yep, look in the mirror and say hello to our new dishwasher."

"What?!?!"

"If you don't have responsibility, you're going to get in trouble," Janice said, "and I don't want you hanging out with those… Castle people," she sneered.

"But the Castle is cool!"

"It's the butthole of this town. Starting tonight, you're on the same schedule as me at The Roost."

"Fuuuh…" I stopped myself half a syllable short.

"Don't you even. Donovan, you're too smart for your own good and without a job, you'll be too bored to do anything smart."

"I earned the right to be bored! I got good grades. I'd rather go to summer school than wash dishes six double shifts a week with my… Why the hell do I have to work?"

"Okay, mister, okay. I want you to go outside, all the way to the front yard, and walk back in. While you are walking, I want you to total up every single item in this house and tell me how much money it is when you reach the back. Then total up the car, gas, insurance, health bills, phone bills, groceries, clothes—all the rest. Now tell me where this money comes from. But maybe you think I pay with magic beans."

I knew we were broke because it was the moat of poverty that kept me from the Castle. Once last summer, I decided I was finally going to get inside. All I needed was three dollars and seventy-five cents. An approachable sum to a normal kid, but a lot to someone who didn't ever have a penny in their pocket.

"I'm not giving you an hour's pay so you can piss your pants!" Janice would say when I asked for money.

So one day while observing the local bums at the pier, I hatched a plan. Less of a plan and more of a plea, really, but still a way to get a ticket. I squatted in front of the Castle and put up a cardboard sign that said, "Homeless. Please Help." People gave me more sympathetic glances than change but after a few hours, I was about halfway there. I kept busy by thinking of techniques to master the puppetry of heart strings. While practicing a trembling lip, I heard a familiar voice scream my name.

"Donovan!" It was the bloodcurdling, wretched shriek of a witch. A voice like this could front a metal band.

"Donovaaaaannnn!" It was Janice across the street, stopping the car in the middle of traffic and ripping her door open. She stormed across the road, dodging cars with a middle finger, and tore the sign out of my hands.

"Is this who we are?! I don't work sixty hours a week for you to be a beggar! Do you realize how many people saw you?"

"But—"

"Get in the car!"

I went to pick up the change in my hat, but Janice hooked my elbow and jerked me away.

"My money!"

Then Janice yelled something at me that was so angry I couldn't even decipher it. This was the most pissed off I had ever seen her. My mom always had a loose grip on her anger at the world but this was way more intense than usual. Janice buttholed her lips, squinted her eyes shut, and dug her nails into my arm as we crossed the busy street. As she sputtered in fiery tongues unknown, I melted into compliance. Cars honked all around us as Janice garbled more nonsense. Her face took the shape of someone who'd eaten a bitter lemon with a fart in it. She held this expression until we pulled in our driveway, where Janice proceeded to unleash hell—phase two.

"Do you have any idea of what you are advertising to the world? What this says about our family?" She sounded like an evil cartoon character.

"I just wanted—"

"I don't know what I did to deserve this. I don't know what to do with you. Do you want to go live with another family? Because I will gladly support that decision. That's what you want, don't you? I don't think they'll take this shit any better. But then you can burn them out and move on to your next failure."

"No, but—"

"That's what this tells me. Well, I'll look into it and see if anyone will take you. I'm not sure."

"I'm sorry."

"Get out."

I got out of the car and went inside. Janice stayed in the car crying for so long that I began to fear what would happen when she got out. When she finally did, Janice parented the only way she knew how—by belt.

I leaned over the sink and closed my eyes. *Crack! Crack! Crack!* Janice would stop for a second to catch her breath and then… *Crack! Crack! Crack!* She had issues but I didn't really know what they were or why I had to pay for them. Sure I was out begging, but the punishment didn't fit the crime. And I was way too old for this to still be going on. The one person who was supposed to protect me was the one beating the shit out of me more than any bully at school. Janice didn't whip the hell out of me. She whipped hell into me.

So then I thought I would destroy the one thing I knew she loved. I went into the living room where she sipped on white wine and watched the TV. I walked up to the TV and kicked it in. Broken glass, a puff of smoke and an electronic fizzle. I couldn't open my mouth to talk because I would have erupted in tears, so I left without a word. The next day she brought home a stack of horror magazines and comic books from the grocery store. I would have rather had a ticket to the Castle but I would take any sign of remorse. It took a while for us to get a new TV, but she never hit me again.

Those marks from years of the belt are still on my ass. You can't see them, but they're there. I stopped calling her "Mom" after too many beltings. "Janice" offered more distance from the nauseating reality that the person who gave birth to me was the person who made me black and blue. She hated it. "It's goddamned creepy that you call me 'Janice'. Especially in front of people who know I'm your mom." All the better then.

But today, a new type of horror was unfolding in the living room. Janice and I stared at each other, each looking for a sign of weakness. I broke the silence.

"So… I'll get paid though, right?"

"Yes, you will get a paycheck."

My eyes lit up.

"But I will be taking it and using it for our family's expenses."

"What?!"

"That's right."

"Family expenses like white wine?"

My only weapon at home was quick wit delivered by a sharp tongue. It was defensive instinct more than a desire to artfully belittle someone. But if I wasn't at least a little defiant, I'd probably be hanging from a rope somewhere. I'd rather have some real friends but since that wasn't happening, I turned my middle finger into a switchblade. Janice had done the same.

"No, family expenses like the hour-long, hot-water masturbation marathon you call a bath."

I was silent.

"We're working tonight. It's Sandy and Julio's anniversary and I said we'd cover it."

"I don't even get an afternoon off?"

"You always say you want to be treated like an adult until that means actually being one."

The Roost was located in a part of town that would sooner be forgotten than turned over. The diner hadn't changed anything but the toilet paper since the sixties. It had a long counter bar and a few booths against the front windows. One good thing was that no one from school would ever see me. Lonely old men were the dominant patrons of The Roost. It was like they all came to ride out the end of the storm together. If they woke up the next morning, they'd show up again and wait for the inevitable at the bar.

I walked into The Roost behind my mom.

"Hey, everybody, meet the new dishwasher, my son," Janice said as she tossed her purse by the coffeepot. Before anyone could respond, she continued, "Alright, enough celebration, get to work. Viktor!"

The short-order cook, Viktor, poked his head through the service window, holding a butcher knife. The heat lamps made his sweaty face sparkle an evil glow. He was a Russian something-something who sought political refuge behind a grill.

"Ya?"

"Get Donovan in the back and working."

"You heard," Viktor said, lowering his brow my way.

I passed through the swinging doors and into the kitchen. Total disaster. Dirty plates, trays, glasses, bowls, utensils—everything piled up in or vaguely around an industrial sink filled with dark-gray water. The floor and walls looked like they'd been hit by a decade-long food fight. In all the years that I had been coming to The Roost, I had only seen Viktor's head through the service window. Always a few orders behind, his husky voice and intense focus projected the image of a towering man with expert knife skills. I didn't expect to find him standing on a footstool with two phone books stacked on top of it so he could reach the grill. His rotund gut was in constant peril of being cooked medium rare whenever he leaned toward the back of the grill.

"Hey," I said, as bummed as possible.

"Hahahaha, look at you."

"What?"

"This," he said, motioning around at the mess. "This is yours now."

"Who normally does the dishes?" I said, looking at the overflowing sink.

Janice yelled from the front for a chicken sandwich with popcorn shrimp.

"No time for chit-chat," Viktor said in his thick accent while throwing a chicken breast on the grill.

"Shit shat?"

"Chit-chat!"

"Shit? Shat?"

"Chit! Chat!"

"It sounds like you're saying shit shat."

"How many languages you speak, Donovan?"

"All of them," I said.

"You want trouble already?"

"It gets worse than this?"

"You see."

Viktor took the hair net off his head and threw it at me. He grabbed a fresh one for himself from a nearby cupboard.

"You wear hair net so you don't get it on food," he said.

"But I'm washing dishes, not cooking."

"I tell you how we work. Work hard, no problem. Work lazy, big problem."

"Okay, but why do I have to wear a hair net if I'm washing dishes? If I get a hair on anything, it'll wash off."

"You have to wear hair net because you have to wear hair net."

"But the only food I'm touching is going in the trash."

"No hairs! If I see black hair, I know it's you."

"Okay, I promise to not go bald while flying over your grill."

"Don't expect breaks because of mamulya," he said nodding to the front.

"If anything, my hair is the cleanest thing back here. At least it's been washed today."

Viktor ignored me. He turned up the classical station on the radio and focused on the chicken breast.

I started whittling away at the dishes. I got bored and picked back up with Victor. "What kind of breaks could there even be? The Roost is like a town gathering of people who haven't gotten a break. That's why they work here or eat this shit."

Viktor smacked the spatula on the grill with a loud clap.

"The break is you don't break." Viktor motioned to the dishes. "That will take one hour if you work hard. Two hours if you act like spoiled honky."

I had never been called a honky before and bit my lip to keep from laughing. I started washing dishes and, almost immediately, let a water glass slip through my fingers. It smashed into more pieces than I thought possible.

Janice burst through the swinging doors.

"Acting out already? Viktor, you have my full permission to keep this boy on track no matter what, okay?"

Viktor flashed a gold tooth at me.

Fuck.

I concentrated on the task at hand. The work was so boring, I strained to think of something to entertain myself with. The only option was listening to people on the other side of the heat lamps. It took some effort to hear over the running faucet and sizzling grill, but most of them wanted to address the whole place anyway.

"I just can't even remember the last time I could have a milkshake. It's been so long."

"Why's that, Ernie?"

"Milkshake in, milkshake out. Know what I mean?"

I shivered and looked over my shoulder to try to spot the lactose intolerance through the service window. It was an old guy sitting between two other old guys. They all looked the same. I had no experience with old people growing up. Janice had cut off communication with relatives since before I was born and never told me why.

Their skin appeared translucent. You could see the veins at different depths and sizes. Wrinkles and Super Bowl–style rings covered their fingers. I imagined they were for stuff like "1972's Western Regional Vacuum Sales Leader." The thought of being a champion salesman made me shiver again. I shouldn't have turned around. It was better to be hypnotized by the circling drain I hovered over.

Afterward, Janice and I went home and performed our nightly ritual of watching TV in silence. The program was about a talking car and a rogue detective. In the middle of a scene showing the car hydroplaning on the ocean, she changed the channel.

"Wait!" I said.

"That show has gone downhill. It's like a cartoon now."

"I think it's even better."

Janice flipped through channels and landed on the tail end of the news. It broke into commercial but not just any.

"Nee ner neeeee!" An organ rang out Bach's "Toccata and Fugue in D Minor." It was seriously my favorite song.

Its thick atmosphere filled the living room as a foreboding voice said, "Castle Dunes is alive again! A living, breathing nightmare of more than thirty incredible rooms, each with its own very special surprise. Wander through the myriad of secret passageways and winding labyrinths. Discover the Throne of the Living Dead and its unimaginable terror. There's Dracula, the Prince of Darkness, and many more. Castle Dunes is waiting for you!"

Images of witches, zombies, and evil druids went along with the foreboding voice and featured Dracula most of all. At the end, he spread his red-lined cape over a hot chick in a nightie and went for her neck.

"That's what I wanna be," I said to an already frowning Janice.

"You can't be Dracula when you grow up. That doesn't even make sense."

"No, like him," I said motioning to the TV.

"No one goes, 'Oh, my son? Well, he's a Dracula. Got a big house on the beach with a big, happy family. Bills? He pays them by scaring people and they just go away. We're all real proud of him.'"

The Dracula stuff had been a sore subject at home for a while. Years ago, I kept wearing a vampire cape after a Halloween that came and never went. Eventually, Janice threw it away instead of washing it. I rushed into the kitchen when I couldn't find it.

"Where's my cape?"

"Cut this shit out. I swear you're just trying to torture me." The cape was embarrassing for any parent but it was compounded with a reminder of Janice's magic past.

That Christmas, Janice asked what I wanted.

"A new cape."

She got me a sweater.

It's not like I wasn't into the other famous monsters, but Dracula was the boss. The Castle was his and the rest were capable only of being guests. Frankenstein was too dumb, Wolfman couldn't control himself, the Mummy took forever, and the Invisible Man wasn't anything to look at. It was Drac who ran shop. With a hypnotizing eye, flight capabilities, and immortality, he had them all beat.

The career conversation went back on mute and I retreated to my room. I fell on the bed and stared at my two Castle Dunes brochures taped to the wall. The full color pamphlets were the same one but folded out to show each side's four panels. The front side was taken up by a giant photo of the Castle with a crowd below. A hand-drawn Dracula loomed over the scene, and a dialogue bubble by his head said, "Castle Dunes! Follow the bats to the pier of fear!"

The other side featured three shots of the pier showing carnival games of skill and chance, the arcade, and food stands like Castle Pizza and I Scream. There was also a coupon for a discount if you bought twelve tickets.

Based on commercials, brochures, and word of mouth, I could only vaguely piece together what the Castle was like inside. But even better than the Castle propaganda were the local legends. It was said that half of the people going through would never come out, and those that did had lost their minds. They said the Castle people would follow you home at night. And that the building had been transported brick by brick from Carpathia. None of which I knew to be true, but the stories were still rad. The Castle was only about a mile down the road but Janice made it seem a world away.

I opened the window to cool off and listened to the neighborhood's silence. Dunes sucked. It was totally fucking boring. We had one movie theater and it only showed one movie at a time. The town's adults were bored enough to actually give a shit about our high school sports. I'd see grown men stop dudes in letterman jackets on the street and talk to them like war heroes. We just had one big grocery store and its produce section constantly sat on the brink of rot. Our main industry seemed based around the liquor stores.

Once a year, Dunes had a Garlic Festival. It never made sense to me. We didn't grow garlic. It all came from about twenty miles inland. And if two shut-down blocks counted as a festival, then you could call the busiest intersection in town a "Traffic Festival." But everyone pretended we were "famous" for our garlic. And once a year, this cloud of bad breath hung over Dunes as our prideful tradition. Fucking garlic. I'm with Dracula on that.

So yeah, Dunes sucked. But Castle Dunes? Ruled. To me, it was the saving grace of both the town and my imagination. It was like, yeah, life's boring and everything sucks, but if you could scale the iron gates of the Castle, you'd escape the pale-gray, slow death of suburban nothingness. Famous monsters never die. And I wanted to get inside more than anything in the world. But the fact that it simply existed gave me enough hope to keep me going. All of the Castle's advertising spoke an overarching, kind of subliminal message to me. It said, "Don't worry about *them*. Join *us*. We want *you*!"

As I stared at the ceiling, a change in the breeze outside carried a faint trail of Bach's "Toccata." Originating from the Castle's outdoor PA system, it found me as it poured over the windowsill and crept through the room. Comforted by the other world's soundtrack drifting into my own, I began to fall asleep.

2

The next day was the hottest on record for that day in Dunes history. When Janice and I walked into The Roost, a rank stench blew past us and out the door. Janice made her signature butthole face and threw her purse at the coffee pot. I couldn't imagine the odor going without remark.

"What the hell is that smell? Did Viktor die on the toilet?" I asked.

"It's the grease trap."

"This place?"

"No, the grease trap. It happens when it's hot out. Get back there and clean it."

I parted the swinging doors and got slammed with origin-strength stench.

Viktor was on his hands and knees under the sink.

"Jesus, is that smell coming from your ass crack?" I said.

"Get down here!"

I got on the floor beside Viktor. He pulled his arm out of a deep hole.

"This is you. Clean grease trap. It catches all grease from dishwater and holds so pipes don't stop."

I let out a deep sigh but could only inhale short breaths to avoid being overtaken by the smell of rotting grease.

"And put on hair net!"

When I finished, my arms were covered in brown grease that wouldn't wash off.

"How am I supposed to clean dishes when I'm covered in slime?"

"Here," Viktor said, throwing a Brillo pad at me.

"This is for stainless steel, not skin!"

"Don't be girl. It will get off."

I worked the pad on my arms and it really did take the grease off. It also took off any hair on my arm and the first two layers of skin. I showed my raw arm to Viktor.

"See? Now stop lazy and start wash."

After a while, I started getting the hang of the dishes but had no pride or pay to show for it. My thoughts turned to a possible escape. Going AWOL from The Roost became a full-time obsession.

While I was scheming to myself over the sink, Janice walked into the back.

"A customer left their dentures on a plate, where are they?"

"Huh?"

"For your own sake, tell me you got them."

"What dentures?"

"Gibby left her dentures on her plate yesterday. You didn't see someone's fucking teeth staring at you while you're doing dishes?"

"There's a lot of dishes."

"So I take that as a no."

"Yes."

"Well, Gibby has been coming here for over twenty years and if she said she left her dentures in a pile of mashed potatoes, we are going to find them for her."

"How do you forget teeth?"

"Well, the good news is you get a break from the kitchen."

"Yeah?"

"Yeah. Because you're going through the dumpster to find her teeth. That you threw out."

"The dumpster!"

"The dumpster!" Janice echoed.

"You told me to never play in dumpsters."

"I didn't say anything about working in them."

I went out to the alley and threw open the filthy dumpster. It was far worse than the grease trap and a hundred times bigger. Parts of it were actually moving, heaving with flies, maggots, and roaches scurrying about. I couldn't do it.

I went back inside, to the front, where Janice was talking with Gibby.

"I'm not going in that thing! It's fucking alive!"

Janice grabbed my arm and dug her fingers in the tendons as she led me into the kitchen.

"Don't you dare talk to me like that. Ever. And especially not in front of customers. You have no class. None." Janice grabbed a napkin and doused it with a bottle of vanilla extract. "Here. Put this in your face and start digging."

"I don't need that—I need a flame thrower!"

Janice made the butthole face and worked her jaw muscles to show that she was gearing up for the rarely seen "other level."

"Fine. But if I die, it's your fault."

"I can live with that." Janice spun around and changed her expression the moment she put her hand on the kitchen door.

I started walking back to the alley but Viktor stopped me.

"Wait. Take these," Viktor said, handing me two unused trash bags.

"What's this gonna do?"

"Put each one on legs and pull drawstring tight by thighs."

"You're pretty cool for a Russian, Viktor."

"Cool is nothing."

I put the trash bag chaps on and waddled outside. I stood in front of the dumpster for five minutes, trying to psych myself up. Finally,

I climbed in and started picking through the rotten debris. All the food that I had scraped off was coming back to haunt me. I plunged my fists through bags of varying consistencies and tried to hold my stomach contents down. What seemed like hours was only fifteen minutes, but I found the dentures with a blind fist. I pulled myself out of the dumpster and slipped on my trash bag legs when they hit the ground—taking the fall on my elbow. I limped inside as a thin layer of blood started to rise to the top of the scrapes.

"Here you go," I said handing the dentures to Gibby. "Some guys tried to steal your teeth but I wouldn't let 'em, so they kicked my ass."

"That's so sweet of you. Thank you so much, Janice." Gibby took her teeth and left.

Janice looked sideways at me.

"Bullshit."

"No, seriously. I should go home, though, don't you think? I mean, if I'm not supposed to get a hair on the dishes, blood probably isn't good either, right?"

"Get in the back before you make people puke." Janice yelled into the service window, "Viktor! Fix him up with the first-aid kit."

"Ya."

I went to the back while Viktor unfolded paper napkins next to a spool of tape.

"Where's the first-aid kit?"

"This," Viktor said, pointing to the napkins and tape. He then reached out from under his apron and revealed a flask. "And this."

"I don't drink."

"No. Come."

Viktor pulled my elbow across the sink.

"What are you doing?"

"Vodka cleans."

"Is it gonna sting?"

"Good vodka won't sting."

He splashed his flask on my elbow.

"Fuck, that stings!"

"I didn't say this was good vodka," he said, taking a swig.

I grabbed a napkin and clutched my arm.

"That would have been me in dumpster if you weren't working. You're okay."

"Whatever."

"Keep this up and you've got real future here," Viktor said, laughing.

The next day, Viktor had diarrhea and kept running from the grill to the toilet. All the food burned on the grill in his absence. Janice pretended to serve the dishes like they were perfect and when the customers voiced their disgust, she acted shocked and appalled. Eventually, she told Viktor if he burned another dish, she'd start throwing them back in his face. So Viktor enlisted me to back him up on his runs.

"Donovan, I need you to cook when I go," he said.

"I don't know how to cook, man."

"It's easy. You put whatever is they order on grill. When starts burning, you flip over. When other side starts burning, you put on a plate with some of this," he said, pointing at a pile of parsley that looked like fake foliage on a model train track.

"Fair enough. But don't leave me hanging."

Viktor clutched his stomach and ran off.

I started doing it just as he said when I quickly got backed up. Janice looked through the service window, saw me managing different piles of burning food, and exploded.

"What in God's name are you doing? Where's Viktor? I'm getting killed out here!"

"He's squirtin' dirt in the toilet," I said, chopping up hash browns and trying to pretend like I had it under control. I didn't have it under control.

"You're ruining everything!"

It wasn't the first time Janice had told me that.

"How long has he been gone?"

"I dunno," I said. I was too busy juggling blackened chicken sandwiches, pretending to know what went inside a Denver omelet, and staying the fuck away from the deep fryer. It was a cauldron of hell that would bubble up and take a bite out of you if you got anywhere near it.

"Well, go get him!" she said, like it was all my fault.

I abandoned the grill and knocked on the bathroom door. No answer. I knocked again. No answer. I yelled his name a few times. No answer. Finally, Janice came and opened the door with her keys. She was still looking at me like this was my fault. When she opened the door, a foul odor poured out and there was Viktor—asleep on the toilet. I started laughing, which pissed Janice off even more. She slapped Viktor's face and he woke up like he didn't know where he was. It made me laugh even more. He hadn't even flushed before falling asleep.

"Jesus Christ, you fucking Russian. You're going to get us closed down."

"Ya ya ya! I'm coming!" he said while getting up, exposing his penis and toilet contents. Janice and I couldn't have turned around fast enough. Still buckling his pants, Viktor returned to the pile I had created and deconstructed my work as if I had explained it all to him in great detail. He was pretty damn good at his job when he wasn't shitting himself to sleep.

The next morning, I awoke to the rooster-precision timing of Janice's screams in the kitchen.

"Donovan!"

She yelled it every morning as if venting her frustration at my existence. Normally, this ritual would be completed with the sound of my door opening and a bathroom flush, or me yelling, "I'm up!" and going back to sleep, which only made things worse. But today I had a different plan.

A third scream barreled down the hallway with Janice and burst into my room.

"Goddamn it! Get. Up."

Janice wasn't a morning person, and having to drag someone else through the first hour of the day never made it better.

A scaly rash had broken out over my arm from the grease trap and gray dishwater.

"Check this rash out. I'm sick, I can't go."

"Pssffft! Viktor's got the flu or a cold or something every other week. People don't stop making dirty dishes just because you're sick. For the last time, up."

"I'm serious. I think I'm gonna barf."

She disappeared. For a moment I thought it was a silent, frustrated goodbye—but seconds later, she came back with a salad bowl and threw it on the bed.

"Here."

"What am I gonna do with this?"

"I'll tell you what you won't do. You won't puke all over my car. Two minutes and we're going."

"I seriously don't think I should go. What if I barf at The Roost?"

"We've got plenty of bowls there too."

I realized it would take more than claiming a fever and possible leprosy to make my summertime dreams come true, so I temporarily relented.

"Okay, let me go to the bathroom."

"Alright, but I don't want to hear any sloppy lotion sounds. Make it quick."

In the bathroom, I opened the medicine cabinet and reached for a small brown bottle, slipping it in my pocket.

As we got in the car, Janice glared at me.

"Where's the bowl?"

"I think I can make it."

"That's what I thought. You look fine. Except for that stupid haircut. Or lack thereof."

"Fuck you and The Roost. This is it," I thought over and over.

I was staring out the window on the way to work when I saw the official Castle Dunes hearse going in the other direction. I had to hide my smile when Janice looked over at me. The hearse had "Follow me to Castle Dunes!" painted on the back and sides in dripping blood. I'd see it around town every now and then. It always felt like the car was a celebrity. I guessed it was the owner's or something. Whoever it was, he seemed like the luckiest dude in all of Dunes. That hearse could have said, "Follow me off a cliff!" and I would have. Especially if it was written in dripping blood.

When we showed up, Viktor was already prepping the day's food.

"Viktor, can you make something for Donovan?"

"Sure, what'll it be?"

"The Trucker Special," I said.

"Wowee, big! Coming up."

Janice looked sideways at me as I felt the act slip. It didn't matter, the plan was in motion.

"What? I'm hungry."

The Trucker Special was the biggest item on the menu. Four eggs, four sausages, four bacon strips, four pancakes, half a pound of hash browns, and two pieces of toast. I don't know why they stopped at the theme of four when they got to the toast.

I sat at the counter while Janice started tending to the regulars.

"More coffee, hon? Some jelly, sweetie?"

I only heard this tone in her voice when I eavesdropped on her at work. These strange regulars were "sweetie"s and "hon"s, and I was an earsplitting scream.

The Trucker Special arrived in front of me without a word from Janice. I began eating the dish chunk by chunk, working my way through sets of four at a steady speed. The struggle came with the pancakes.

I shoved as many breakfast items as I could into my mouth and quickened the pace when Janice turned her back. I could tell she was beginning to sense something was up when she shot a look across the counter.

"What do you think you're doing?"

My mouth was too full to answer. I tried to respond but egg yolk ran down my chin and I flashed the rest with an open smile.

Some old guy said, "Boy's gotta eat. Sure didn't get to be six foot five on Cracker Jacks."

Janice patronized him with a smile.

A man staring at his oatmeal added, "Wish that was me. Last time I got that plate was over ten years ago and I think parts of it are still inside me."

Everyone stopped to pay attention to the last detail. The man tried to cover his tracks with a hearty cough followed by a "'Scuse me."

"I'd like to bet he can't finish the rest in three minutes," another old guy chimed in.

I ate and ate until I had one final stab of pancake, sausage, egg yolk, and syrup left. Janice fixed her eyes on me as I devoured the last bite.

"Okay, now get to work."

"Can I have a water?"

"Jesus."

Janice turned around to the service station and poured a glass of water from the pitcher. At the same time, I slipped my hand into my pocket and brought the small vial out from underneath the counter. It was ipecac, the medical world's solution for inducing vomit. I unscrewed the top and thanked Janice for the water. I faked like I was coughing as I downed the entire vial, chasing it as fast as I could with the ice water. The desired effect began rumbling in my stomach way sooner and more intense than I thought it would.

"Hunnnnggaaaaaah!" Vomit exploded out of my mouth in all directions. Every bite I had just taken was now painting the counter and the walls, and splattering nearby patrons of The Roost.

"Oh, God, it's on my legs!" one of the regulars yelled.

"What the hell?!" Janice screamed as she ran to the back for a bowl.

I had never taken ipecac before, so I didn't really know what happened other than that it made you barf. That was happening, yes—but to my increasing horror, it wasn't stopping.

I didn't know what to do with myself. Even if I did I wouldn't be able to do anything amid the flood coming out. Janice returned with a large bowl. When I looked up from my hands and knees, I puked again—covering the bowl, Janice's apron, and her shoes.

The scene was too much for the regulars to stomach. Utensils fell loudly to their plates. People bumped their tables trying to get up and away. They yelled things like "Land's sakes!" and "My word!" or "Heavens to Betsy!"

I could only look up for brief snapshots before returning to my own puddle, unable to halt the process I brought on myself. I had blown through the Trucker Special and was beginning to see bits from days ago. The skeletal remains of lettuce. An "X" and "Y" from alphabet soup. A sausage pellet.

By now, I was struggling to get enough air when I lost my grip on the vial I was hiding. Janice saw it fall to the floor and grabbed it.

"Ipecac! You little shit!"

"Janice, your boy's sick." Don, a regular, stood up for me. "Go eas—ah, God, the smell!" and before Don could finish his defense, he ran outside and disappeared.

"He took ipecac! It makes you do this!" Janice was now on the "other level." "Get out! I never want to see you again!"

My strength was gone, but I managed to make it to the door while dry heaving and burping up pink and yellow spit.

"You bastard!" Janice yelled as she threw my empty plate past me, shattering the glass door and sending me tumbling into the parking lot.

3

I wandered down the road with a quivering gut. My shirt was stained with a V-shape of puke from my neck down. I wiped my slimy hands on the grass by the side of the road and belched an encore. My guts were hollow but I felt bigger. Finally something came up from my stomach that wasn't puke. Pride.

"I'm free," I thought, even though I knew that freedom would only last until later tonight—when I'd have to go home. The home provided by the place I'd just flooded with vomit. I told myself I could sit there and trip out about it or I could keep walking away. "Had to be done," I told myself. "Fuck The Roost."

I checked every pay phone I came across for change. Nothing. I looked up the road and saw the new Castle Dunes billboard, in the same spot every year. The sign always featured a more terrifying, decayed version of Dracula than the year before, pointing the way down the street with one hand and beckoning you closer with the other. "Castle Dunes! More screams! More gore! More terror than ever before!" it read in dripping letters.

The three seventy-five for a Castle ticket stressed me out. I knew where I was going, I just didn't know what I'd do once I got there. I wasn't sure if I could solve my problems by going to the Castle but I could definitely escape them. And since I was already living in the moment today, a temporary escape was a completely credible solution.

I'd spent past summers watching droves pour through the Castle gates and swore that the legend was true—fewer people came out the back than went in. I wanted to be one of the people that was never seen at the exit. Last summer, I saw a girl I liked from school go in. I immediately went to the back of the Castle, from where the rest of the pier extended, and waited for her. Would she come out giggling with her friends with attention-grabbing fake screams or would she be drenched in tears? I figured, somehow, I'd get to the bottom of her cool.

But she never came out. I sat there for two hours and recognized some terrified faces from the ticket line but not hers.

The next school year, I approached one of her friends.

"Hey, whatever happened to Tiffany?"

"Ew, get away." She was not impressed with the guy-wearing-a-cape-and-asking-about-her-friend combo.

"Is she dead?" I said, really trying to be sensitive about it.

"What is the matter with you?!"

"I'm really sorry," I said while maintaining a respectful tone about her passing.

"Her parents moved up north."

"'Cause she died in the Castle?"

"Oh my God, you're such a frickin' weirdo."

Later that night, I asked my mom if the Castle killed people who went through it. She said, "Yes."

I no longer thought the Castle killed people but I didn't put it past the place. The closer I walked to it, the louder I could hear the "Toccata." When I arrived in front of the Castle, I hit the same bench where I sat every year and gazed at the dominating structure. It projected a glow of ominous strength. Its giant, iron gates separated me from the "living, breathing nightmare!" that was my dream. Behind the gates stood five towering stories of stone and mortar. Looking closer at the exterior, I noticed some damage to the fake masonry. There were now exposed patches of plywood and drywall where the building's foundation met the sand. Last winter, a pretty brutal storm rolled through Dunes and the Castle's much-needed repairs went ignored. I hadn't been to the pier since it opened for the summer. I took a deep breath and soaked up its cool shadow. It was still early in the day and not many people were around yet. I was at evil-themed peace.

After a while, I got up and checked out the rest of the pier for new stuff. Extending out behind the Castle, the pier was packed with an array of games and junk food. I went over to the arcade, Circuit Circus, to watch people play games. Two older teens were playing one called Joust and drank from oversized soda cups they kept at their feet. I walked up behind them.

"Take off, dude. We've got this all day," the tall, blond one said, nodding to the row of quarters lined on the bottom of the screen. I stopped counting them after twelve.

"I just want to watch."

"Jesus Christ, is that your breath? Get the fuck out of here," said the stockier one with a buzz cut.

He reached for his soda between rounds and took a big pull.

"Dude, I gotta piss," he said.

"Yeah, me too. Hey, we'll let you watch us play if you guard our spot real quick." The blond dude made it seem like a threat.

"Okay."

"Don't lose our spot."

The two dudes left for the bathroom while I looked over their game. And money.

At least sixteen quarters. At least. Sixteen divided by four is four. Four dollars right there. Three seventy-five to get into Castle Dunes...

I looked around and didn't see anyone paying attention. I cupped one hand under the row of quarters and slid my finger across the bottom of the screen in one sweeping motion. With a fistful of coins and sweat, I ran out of the arcade, past the carnival games, and straight to the Castle ticket counter.

A frowning girl in white face paint, blackened eyes, and a druid robe sat behind steel bars separating tickets from customers.

"One ticket, please."

She counted the quarters in impatient silence, tore off a ticket, and threw it at me with the change. I let the change roll down the entrance ramp as I ran up through the iron gates.

Another pale-faced, druid-robed employee took the ticket from my trembling hand and tore it with his teeth—spitting the other half back at me and swallowing the rest.

This was already awesome.

I was ushered into a foyer-type room that had a fake fireplace with a portrait of Dracula above the mantel. Even though it was dark, you could tell the room details were kind of dingy. A small group of customers, young and old, was already gathered in front beneath the portrait. The druid at the door closed it and the lights went out.

A recording came on with sounds of crashing thunder and rain. In a flash of strobe lights, the actual Dracula appeared where the portrait had just been. The small crowd screamed and hollered. It was him, the Dracula from the commercial. He had on the same frilly, white Victorian shirt with the medallion swinging from his neck. There were some changes though. His hair wasn't entirely black. He had about a quarter-inch of blond roots showing and now looked too buff to be evil. Dracula pounced onto the mantel and whipped his cape at the crowd.

"We've been expecting you!" he said in a bad Transylvanian accent. It was hilarious even though I was expecting to be scared. But it wasn't just terror I came for, this stuff also made me laugh. Shitty or great, it was all horror to me and I loved it.

"Allow me to introduce myself. I am the Prince of Darkness, the King of Castle Dunes, and the last thing you may ever see! You may call me Dracoooolya. Kneel at my throne that is Castle Dunes and obey these rules!"

My jaw hung in anticipation. It was awesome but not what I'd expected. Dracula comes out and tells you rules?

"First, keep your hands and feet to yourself or you might not get them back. Second, do not touch my stuff. I killed a lot of people to afford this place—and I don't need you messing it up. Third, if any of you ladies are wearing perfume on their neck, please wash it off. I do hate the taste. Go now, before I get hunnnngry," he said, eyeballing a girl in the front.

I thought my face was going to shatter from smiling so much. Dracula couldn't miss me in the crowd and interpreted it as mockery.

"And you! I promise we will meet again and I'll wipe that smile off your living face."

Dracula disappeared behind the mantel in a *poof* of smoke, thunder, and strobes. A druid ushered the group through a hidden door that led to the rest of the self-guided tour.

From the first room on, nothing was watered down. Evil things jumped out at me from crusty jail cells, graveyards, and mazes. I was stoked by its full-on approach. Gore dripped from decapitated heads, zombie guts spilled out of their chests, upside-down crosses were planted on nuns' faces, and gallons of blood red paint ran down the Castle's brick walls throughout.

I got to one room where two female vampires were sitting on a bed covered with red silk sheets, holding hands. They claimed to be Dracula's lovers.

"Oh! You're handsome. I'm sure Dracula wouldn't mind if we had just a little snack."

"Me first!" the other said.

The women stretched their arms at me and begged me to stay for "just a bite." I soaked up their pleas until it got awkward and they looked at me weirdly while trying to maintain character.

"Don't just stand there, die with us or leave!"

I couldn't believe that hot, monster chicks were possibly hitting on me, act or no act. They even gave me an ultimatum that included the option of staying. I left and promised myself I'd be back. On the way out, I heard one of them ask, "Was that puke on his shirt?"

A lot of the rooms didn't have real people in them. There were many set-piece rooms filled with homemade mannequins, like the medieval torture chamber with slightly out-of-proportion executioners, frozen in the position of delivering a death blow to crying maidens. Rooms featured mannequins tied to racks, group hangings, and dead babies in jars. I stopped at the executioner scene and let the rest of the group go ahead of me so I could wander alone.

The craftsmanship of the executioners sucked and was awesome at the same time. I examined the rushed details of the brutes' faces and the sloppy airbrushing. It made them so much more appealing than the most ornate headstone in Odd Fellows Cemetery. I waited for the screams ahead of me to trail off and walked alone.

I came to a room with a gold-framed, oval-shaped mirror hanging on the wall. When I walked in front of it, there was no reflection of me—just the empty room behind me. I stood before it as the lights dimmed and sounds of thunder filled the room. An unnaturally low, wizardy voice began speaking through a recording.

"I am the Mirror of Death and as I have looked through others who have come before you—so do I look into your life." Thunder crashed again and the voice continued, "You seem to pass through life always seeking something just beyond your reach. You have not been aware of this evasive goal, just of an inner rebellion and restlessness against your lot."

I looked around the empty room. This mirror was taking some pretty personal leaps.

"You have felt that evil or bad luck surrounded you and held you back. This is an alibi for your own shortcomings. Go now... and wander the darkened halls of Castle Dunes... and find power."

The lights came back on and I cupped my hands around my eyes and leaned into the mirror. It was a plastic windowpane that separated me from an identical room on the other side, creating the illusion that I had no reflection. I thought it was a cool trick and wondered what other dark fortunes you could get. As I studied the untouched, cleaner version of the room I was in, an actor dressed as a rotting skeleton popped up in front of the mirror from below.

"Ahhhh!" We both screamed at the same time but for different reasons. The skeleton pointed at me as he lowered himself back down behind the mirror.

It fed my excitement to keep moving through rooms. I needed more so I could keep the horror high going. Many of the longer room-to-room transitions in the Castle were in pure blackness. You just had to learn there was a winding staircase by tripping over it. Long hallways of nothingness led you face first into a wall. I climbed another flight of dark stairs and opened a door, revealing the roof of the Castle and a catwalk to another door back inside.

On the catwalk, I could see the whole town on the land side and the beach on the other. People played in the ocean and laid out on the sand. I turned around and looked for my house. I saw the flagpole a couple blocks from where we lived and guesstimated the distance to my house. Looking down at the treetops of my home, I never imagined the Castle could provide such a perspective.

A scared group of girls ran into me.

"Get out of the way!" they yelled.

"Hey, that's my house," I pointed out to one of the girls.

"Ew," she said as they left the catwalk. I heard them screaming immediately on the other side of the door and smiled.

I spent more time on the roof of the Castle than I had in any room before it. The sound of the ocean mixed with the "Toccata" provided the perfect horror fan's relaxation. The beach never looked so cool and the town never looked so small.

After a few minutes, I opened the next door inside and was engulfed in darkness as my eyes readjusted. I made my way through more rooms and crept around cautiously. I came into an old tavern set where a guy dressed as Satan poured drinks for mannequin monsters.

"Do you believe in God?" Satan said, grinning in a demonic voice.

"Why?"

"Do you. Believe. In. God?"

"Wha. Aye," I said in syllables that didn't exist.

"Yes or no. A simple question for a simple human."

"I dunno."

"When you die, where are you going?"

"Never thought about it," I lied.

"So you really don't believe in God?"

"Depends on what you mean by 'God.'"

Satan dropped the schtick.

"Jesus, kid. You're fuckin' blowing it. You're supposed to say, 'Yes,' and then I say, 'Well you're in the wrong place.' For fuck's sake."

"That's pretty cool."

"Get the fuck outta here," Satan said, nodding me out of the tavern.

At the Castle's end, I got chased down the exit hallway by a mad butcher yelling, "Please stay for dinner! You're the main course!" Immediately, I wanted to turn back and start it all over again. In triumph, I threw the exit doors open and stumbled into blinding daylight. Out on the pier, I squinted and rubbed my eyes to readjust. The Castle felt like one blurry, fast-forward tour of a lo-fi hell, peppered with cheesy puns ("Fangs for stopping by!"). No matter how many times I had fantasized about what lay beyond its iron gates, I couldn't have imagined it would've been this rad.

As my pupils dilated in the sun, I spotted the dudes whose quarters I'd stolen. They were harassing some kids about whether they'd seen "a tall fuck-face." Before I could hide, they had picked up on my beaming smile coming out the back gates where others usually scream.

"Motherfucker!" the blond dude yelled.

"There he is!"

The two dudes leapt into action and charged at me as I took off running.

"You can't out-run me!" said the blond, tearing off his jacket to reveal a track and field shirt. I ran out in front of the Castle and down to the beach, hoping to lose him under the pier. But I didn't account for the dry sand. It slowed me down and drained my energy while the runner closed in.

"You are dead! I'm gonna get you!" he yelled, accelerating his pace.

In the slow traction of the sand, I started to realize this might be true. After surviving the horrors of Castle Dunes, I was about to lose my life to something far more boring. Blondie was so close behind me that I could hear his runner's scientific huff and puff. I booked it as best I could to the stretch of beach where the cement fire pits began as I came to grips with the fact that I wouldn't win this race. When the dude went to grasp my shirt, I dropped to the ground and curled into a human speed bump. The dude didn't have a second to react. He tripped over me, just as I'd planned it.

But it sent him flying face first onto the cement edge of a fire pit, as I hadn't planned it. You could hear the bone crunch over the "Toccata."

"Arrrrggggghhhh!"

I looked up and saw Blondie's bloody face rise from the pit and fall back down.

"Oh shit," I said.

Blood was streaming from his nostrils and a couple teeth were missing.

I stood up and just stared at him.

"Get… help…" he said.

The stocky friend caught up to us and ran over to the pile of his friend. He looked from Blondie to me, back and forth, as I got ready to accept the blow of vengeance.

"You're fucking crazy, man." He took caution to stay away from me and circled the fire pit from the other way around.

"Holy shit, dude. Are you okay?" he asked his friend.

"No… Find my tooth… teeth. And… kick his ass." The guy was gonna live but his summer of catching chicks was over.

"What should I do first?"

"Kill him!"

The stocky guy turned to me.

"Let's go, motherfucker!"

He pushed me to the sand. I was now at eye-level with the blond, whose face looked worse than anything I just saw in the Castle. It was too real. Too detailed.

"You're gonna pay for that shit, bad," his friend said.

I looked up at the stocky attacker and braced myself until the suspense was broken by a voice.

"Hey, fuckers!" a voice yelled from behind us.

I watched as the stocky guy turned around and got a one-two combination of having soda poured on his head and getting knocked out with one punch. The guy collapsed, revealing a Mexican-looking metalhead about the same age as me, outfitted with long hair, a patch-covered denim vest, and denim shorts. No shirt. He was smoking a joint and had one checkered slip-on shoe and one black one.

His swing had immediately taken this dude down. I wondered how a lightweight guy like this could take out a bigger one so easily. Then I noticed the sun gleam off his right hand. Brass knuckles.

The metalhead reached a hand out to help me up.

"Hey, bro, I'm Renaldo."

"Hey. Donovan. Thanks for the help."

"No problem, bro. I got all your guys' backs at the Castle, man—it's a war zone in there. Were they pissed you scared them or what?"

"Oh, I don't work there. I just went through it."

"Ah, you're a plebe." He pronounced it "pleeb."

"Huh?"

"You just said you went through the Castle, right?"

"Yeah."

"That's a plebe. The people who go through the Castle. It's what they call 'em, anyway."

"Who?"

"The monsters 'n shit."

"Oh."

"Well, you look like you work there," Renaldo said.

This time I took it as a compliment.

"So what'd you do, then?"

"Uh, I kinda stole their quarters from the arcade so I could go through the Castle."

"Ha! Whatever, man. Fuck jocks! Heavy metal for life."

"Yeah…" After saving me, he could have said, "Smooth jazz for life," and I would have agreed.

"So how was the Castle?"

"I want to live there."

"Rad. First time?"

"Yeah. Have you been?"

"Fuckin' hell yeah, I have, man! Tons of times. Not yet this summer though. I'm waiting for a fully staffed Saturday night so I can get all fucked up and grab some ass! In the dark, dude, it's heaven. You should come, bro."

Invitations were rare for me.

"That'd be cool but I don't have any money. Like, ever."

"Man, come with me and I'll show you how to make money all day."

Renaldo and I walked under the pier to the other side of the beach.

"Check it out, employee entrance," he said.

I thought I knew every detail of the Castle's exterior but I had never noticed this side ramp alongside the pier, or even thought about where the Castle monsters punch in.

"So check this out, man. One of the rules for people that work at the Castle is that they are not allowed to walk around the pier in costume, so on their breaks they come out here on the side, smoke ciggies 'n shit, and have us do food runs for 'em. And, dude, they let you keep the change. That's the deal!"

"Whoa."

"Yeah and it adds up. Look at me!"

"What do you mean?"

"Dude, all my patches, right?! I got 'em by getting Cokes and nachos for the monsters!"

"Oh, cool, how much do they cost?"

"Well, I use the money to buy three darts for a dollar on the pier and then if my dart hits the balloon, I score a patch. Usually, I do—unless it's the end of the night, and there's, like, four balloons left on the wall. Or I'm drunk. That's why I like to play in the morning. *Bam! Bam! Bam!* Patch! Patch! Patch!"

"What if you just bought them?"

"Dude, you can't buy 'em. You have to win 'em. Get it? Come on, I'll introduce you."

We walked up the ramp where four picnic tables were. A zombie druid sat on one, smoking a cigarette, while three witches chatted away at another. A couple kids not affiliated with the Castle stood around the perimeter, watching their every move.

I recognized one of the witches. She worked in the dungeon, and when I had walked in the room, she said I was cute before heading in on some rhyming witches' incantation. Being called cute was more terrifying than the incantation for me. But now here she was, eating a churro and talking to a friend about how she wanted to "slay" some dude tonight.

Renaldo pushed his way past the ogling kids and addressed the employees on break.

"'Sup, everybody, this is Donovan. He's now available for any food runs this summer. Need anything?"

The zombie druid said, "I'll take a churro." It was a different voice than I'd heard in the Castle. Gone was the demonic rasp, and in its place was a dopey drawl. It was moody, but not in the haunted Castle sense—moody like a teenager who was denied a seat at the witches' table.

"Okay, cool," I said.

"Here's two bucks."

The druid handed me the money. I looked to Renaldo, who nodded in approval.

"You witches need any shit?" Renaldo asked.

They shook their heads.

"Cool, we'll be back."

"Better," said the druid.

Renaldo led me up to the pier.

"Dude, churros are a total score! You got a good one."

"Right on."

We walked up to the churro stand and Renaldo pointed at the menu.

"Buck twenty-five, dude. See what I mean?"

"Uh, no."

"Dude, you can make seventy-five cents on this if he gives you the change! This is way better than getting a nacho order, 'cause that shit is a dollar ninety-five. Five cents sucks! So, you hope they get a Coke or something to get away from the nineties or eighties shit."

"Like, offset the math."

"Huh?"

"Like it's 'Wheel of Fortune' but in the other direction."

"Sure, dude."

I returned with the churro.

"Here ya go. And seventy-five cents."

"Keep it," the druid said.

"Thanks."

One of the witches piped up.

"Hey, I want one of those."

"Nice."

I took the money from the witch and walked back to the churro stand with Renaldo. He was going on about how successful he'd been at the operation. This guy just saved me from getting my ass kicked, dropped a dude in one punch, and then rooted me in the underground economy of Castle Dunes. Within minutes, he'd basically saved my life twice. Renaldo shared his secret knowledge of a private kingdom and asked nothing in return. I didn't know how I could ever repay him.

"Dude, aren't you worried about the competition? You know, another guy thinning out the tips?" I said.

"Nah, dude. I sell weed too."

⁓

From afternoon until closing at midnight, I did food runs for the zombies, witches, and assorted ghouls. During the day, I watched monsters rub their eyes and eat ice cream. As the night went on, their appetites changed. Instead of snacks and soda, they repurposed their cups, passed around a bottle, and smoked Renaldo's weed.

During a slow patch toward the end, I went out on the pier to look at the Castle at night. High school football field–style lights were rigged up around the perimeter of the Castle to show it off. I stared at the full-moon glow of the three pole-mounted grids and noticed clouds of insects swarming around the lights. The dense, frantic swarm was occasionally penetrated by dive-bombing bats looking for dinner. The real bats came from all around but most of them lived under the pier during the day. They added to the authenticity of the Castle Dunes experience, but the bat shit everywhere did not. Eventually, the grid lights shut off for the night and the swarm scattered.

Renaldo came up to me.

"See ya tomorrow?" he asked.

"If I'm still alive," I said.

"What's up?"

"I think I've got trouble waiting at home. Mom shit."

"Yeah, I hear that," Renaldo said.

"I don't know, man."

"Dude, whenever I think my dad is going to kick my ass, I just go kick my own ass first."

"You kick your own ass?"

"Pretty much. If I'm really drunk, I can take a blow to the face. But if not, I'll just do some insane skate move that I know won't end up good."

"Dude."

"Then when I walk in the door, he's like, 'Who kicked your ass? I'll buy 'em a drink.' Or 'Who kicked your ass? Tell 'em thanks.' Or 'This one's for them,' and he takes a slug. Or 'Call me next time so I can watch.'"

"Fuck, dude."

"Yeah, whatever. Master of destiny, bro."

It might have been wrong but I relaxed hearing someone else's more brutal tales from home.

"How do you deal with it?"

"Man, I'm high all day, every day. I'm so high you can't fucking touch me. You think you're beating the shit out of me. But I'm not even there. Total locust, bro. Kissin' the sky. Everyone looks like ants where I'm coming from."

I didn't know what to say.

"I don't mean you, I mean…" he said.

"Yeah."

"Anyways, catch ya lates," Renaldo said.

"Cool."

Renaldo skated off and I walked home. His stratospheric detachment was something I could relate to. Especially after looking out on Dunes while up on top of the Castle. Heavy thoughts in high places.

The metallic sloshing of all the new change in my pockets made me sound like I was wrapped in chains. By the time I strolled past Odd Fellows Cemetery, I had to hold my belt loops up because of all the weight in my pockets.

I made it home and saw through the window that the living room light was still on. My stomach knotted as I walked in. Janice sat on the couch, drinking wine. She didn't take her eyes off the TV or make any movement acknowledging my arrival.

"Hey…" I said.

Janice let out a deep sigh and stayed fixed on the TV.

"I don't want to work at The Roost anymore."

"You made your point." She took a sip of wine, eyes still on the TV. Janice went to set the wineglass on the coffee table but missed. The glass hit the beige carpet. She didn't notice or didn't care and still hadn't blinked. I watched the clear wine soak into the beige carpet. Is this why she drank the white kind?

"I got a new job." I held out two fists overflowing with change. Janice glanced at my fists and back to the TV. Somewhere hiding on her face was surprise.

"It's at the Castle."

Janice reached for her wine that wasn't there. She got off the couch, went to the kitchen, and came back with another. She gulped half of it down as tears lined up in her eyes.

"I get food for the people that work inside. They usually let me keep the change."

"Sounds like a beggar at a shit hole," she said at the TV.

"You mean what you do at The Roost?"

As soon as I said it, I felt terrible. I shouldn't have gone for a death blow.

Janice turned the TV up like she was turning me down and returned to the other half of her wine in unruffled silence.

My line would have normally inspired a nuclear retaliation, leaving nothing but a burn mark where our house once stood. But tonight, she was entirely expressionless.

I went to bed thinking that my mom had actually given up on me. The feeling was worse than getting yelled at. This catatonic wrath was far more effective. Earlier, I might have thought it meant some sort of freedom. "She doesn't give a shit, so I can do whatever"–type of thing. The puking incident at The Roost was a legendary act but she didn't even mention it. At least it inspired a reaction in the moment. But to get none here made me feel like a ghost in my home. The idea of haunting a place without a spooky brochure didn't feel the same. I opened a window and lay on the bed with the Castle's "Toccata" still echoing in my head. It told me to brush my problems off. No matter what was going on, it didn't matter. The Castle door had opened just enough.

4

When I woke up the next morning, Janice was already gone. The wineglass from the floor was put back in the cupboard. Normally, a box of cereal sat out waiting for me with a carton of milk, a bowl, and a spoon. This was the first day it wasn't there. I quickly gave it a "Whatever" and headed out the door toward the Castle.

When I showed up at the side entrance, Renaldo was already there, smoking a cig.

"Donovan! What's up, man? You look bummed."

"Ah it's nothin', just…"

"Mom shit, huh?"

"Yeah."

"Well, dude, no offense, honestly, but who gives a fuck? You shouldn't. I don't. No point worrying about that now. Take a look around—it's Friday at the pier and the weather is killer. That means two things: chicks aaannnd… chicks! Get ready to rock, motherfucker!"

I gave Renaldo a funny look.

"I mean mother… Just like, dude, fuckin' A!"

We hung out at the base of the pier and waited for the first Castle workers to call us up the ramp and place an order. We traded turns getting the orders while shooing away any competition, which was pretty easy since they were mostly younger kids, easily intimidated by a flash of Renaldo's brass and my height.

The requests were all the same for the most part until the most "famous" member of the Castle, Dracula, came out of the back door. Wearing sunglasses, he strode past the tables and sat at an empty one. He was a local celebrity from being in the Castle commercial but carried himself like a national one. After being immortalized on TV, I learned that Dracula's head swelled up and he abandoned his big-city actor dreams in favor of dominating this one. He had some sort of actor clout at the local community college but never outgrew it, becoming forever drunk on low-level power, semi-hot chicks, and on-the-job liquor.

I was the only runner around and Dracula waved me over like it was the third time he had done so.

I walked over, stoked to work in some small talk and maybe hang out.

"Hey, man, what's up?" I said.

"I need some fucking nachos."

Dracula didn't even look directly at me.

"Sure, man," I said, waiting for him to provide the money.

Dracula stared at me.

"What?" he said.

"I need the money."

"Ugh, God. Here." He threw two dollars on the ground that started to blow away.

I chased after them and filled the order.

When I came back, Dracula examined the nachos closely.

"You passed the test."

"What's that?"

"You didn't spit in my nachos," he said, taking a bite.

If that's all it took to gain his favor, I figured this dude could be pretty cool. I handed Dracula the leftover nickel. He pocketed it and looked me in the eye.

"Can I trust you with something?"

"Yeah, totally."

"It's a very important task and holds a lot of responsibility."

"No problem. I'm your guy."

Dracula pulled out a ten-dollar bill.

"I need a fifth of Jack Daniel's and some condoms."

Holy shit. My mouth hung open.

"Can you handle that?"

"Uh, yeah, I guess," I barely said. I was too starry eyed by fame and intimidated by an impossible task.

"I'm not giving you ten bucks for some 'I guess.'"

"Yeah. Yes. I can do it."

"I need them quick, so move your ass," Dracula said, standing up. He was much shorter than me and visibly bothered by it. "And don't fuck with the Count," he said, whipping his cape around as he headed to the back door.

"No, sir." I had never, ever called anyone "sir" in my entire life and it felt strange that it came out now.

Dracula disappeared back into the Castle. I walked down the ramp and found Renaldo smoking at the bottom.

"Dude."

"What's up? You look like you just saw a ghost," he said.

"Dude."

"Uh, a ghost with big titties?"

"Dude, no. Wait, have you seen one of those?" I asked.

"Spit it out already."

"Dracula came out."

"Which one?"

"Huh?"

"There's like a couple, dude."

"Dracula! The one in the commercial."

"Oh yeah, Colin Dixon," Renaldo deadpanned. "What'd he want, booze?"

"Yeah. And condoms."

"That dude is such a dick, he needs a condom for his whole fucking body."

"How am I supposed to get that shit?"

"You're on your own with that one, man. I can't go into any liquor store within ten miles of here."

"How come?"

"The monsters always want booze once they get rolling, and they'll give you more than the change. Tip a couple bucks, actually, and maybe a can or a pull off a bottle, but I got greedy with it, dude."

"What do you mean?"

"Well, like, you have to buy nachos and churros, right? You can't go behind the counter and steal chips and cheese and jalapeños, right?"

"Yeah…"

"Well, dude, you can totally fucking steal beer. And I would. But I wouldn't tell that to the dude who asked me to get it. So he'd give me ten bucks and I'd just pocket it, steal the beer, and also get tipped. It was great while it lasted."

"Whoa."

"Yeah, so I can't even try that anymore. Last time I did, I walked into the store and was checking out the soda, getting ready to inch over to the beer… when fuckin' *wack*! Some asshole buried a baseball bat in my head. Fuck. That."

"Dude, I'm not gonna steal beers. I can't even run that fast, you know."

"Bro, you're tall enough to get away with it. Buy that shit. Just act old."

"What does that even mean?"

"You know, be, like, tired and complain about how much everything sucks and that you're getting your ass kicked out there."

"Out there?"

"Or you could get a fake ID. I know a dude."

"I need the stuff in an hour or two."

"Just go for it, man. The tall thing is gonna work, I swear."

"What if I get carded?"

"Then ask him if he takes business cards."

"I don't have that either, dude."

"Dude, you're missing the point. Just go over to Liquor World by Naugles, that dude's kinda easy."

"What about the condoms?"

"They have those too."

"I mean, like, how do I get those?"

"Wait, what?"

I threw my arms up in the air.

"Dude, are you a virgin?"

I shot him a "duh!" look followed by a mental retreat to protect myself from a coming attack.

"Ohhh. No, no. It's cool. I don't mean it like that, I just… never mind, dude. They will sell those to you, easy."

"Dude, I'll be embarrassed as hell!"

"Why?"

"It's fucking condoms!"

"Bro, if you're buying condoms it means that they're going on your dick and into a pussy. Buying condoms is, like, going up to the counter all, like, 'Tonight's gonna be one of those hot nights, woo!'" Renaldo said.

I furrowed my brow while processing this.

"Dude, don't worry. If the guy is acting weird, it's probably just because his dick is stuck behind a counter all night."

"Okay," I said as I cut myself off from actually thinking the condoms were for me.

"Don't be embarrassed to be a badass."

I left the Castle pier and walked down the street to the liquor store. When I got there, I stood outside and tried to see past the beer signs and lottery advertisements to get a look at who I would have to face. No one was there. A chime went off and made me jump when I walked into the store. It almost felt like a trap that no one was behind the counter. I thought about Renaldo's beer run tactic and how I could pull off the perfect crime right now. Maybe it was even a setup? I couldn't bring myself to seize the moment. I stuck to the plan.

And fuck the tall thing. How's that gonna work? I made my way to the condoms first. I had never even really stared a box of condoms in the eye before. The sexual innuendos on the packaging made it seem like chicks were just begging for these condoms. I had never thought about how bad chicks wanted sex. It always sounded like something you got away with or that they would just put up with. But this box of condoms was telling me they were actually for "her pleasure." There was a whole other side to this that I hadn't thought about.

I was getting too hung up on reasons not to go for it. This isn't going to work, I'm sixteen! I thought about returning empty handed, then finally gathered enough courage to reach out for a random brand. Just as I put my hand on them, an Asian man came out from the back with a porn mag tucked under his arm. Scared the fucking crap out of me. He nodded and just casually returned the magazine to the rack.

"Hey," he said.

My eyes and hand darted away from the rubbers. I pretended I was more interested in the petroleum jelly and chapstick next to them. After I'd spent what anyone would think was a reasonable amount of time judging the different flavors of chapstick, I went back to looking at the condoms. I remembered Renaldo's advice and reached for whatever brand was closest to my hand.

I browsed around the store for a little until I stiffly walked over to the liquor shelf. From the corner of my eye, I saw the liquor store employee pick up another mag from the rack and lean back in his chair. The clerk peered over the naked women just enough to observe me. His eyes constantly refocused their gaze as they moved between the mag and the liquor shelf.

I wiped my sweaty hands on my jeans and reached for the bottle. With condoms in one hand and booze in the other, I felt the intimidating power of these forbidden objects and got my "old" act together.

"Hey, fucking shitty day, huh?" I said.

"I dunno, been locked up in here."

"I heard that."

"What?"

"It's a slaughterhouse out there."

"What is?"

"Man, I'm just dog tired, ya know?"

The clerk punched in the prices for the items. My heart was racing as fast as my thoughts.

He didn't even ask for my ID! Renaldo was right! I guess the height and the old thing really does help.

"That'll be… oh, wait—can I see your ID?"

I froze.

"ID."

"Do you take business cards?"

The employee laughed and took the bottle off the counter.

"Still want these?" he said, nodding to the condoms.

"Uh, okay."

"Dollar seventy-five. Want a receipt?"

"No, thanks."

"Here you go."

The clerk put the condoms in a bag and handed them over.

"Hey, can I ask you a question?"

"Shoot."

"What gave it away?"

"You browsed the candy aisle for ten minutes."

"Oh. Yeah…"

I grabbed the condoms and quickly walked out.

I went another mile down the road until I got to St. Helen's Liquor. It was an old man working this time. I needed to turn down the candy browsing and crank up the old thing. Maybe get some camaraderie going. I grabbed the bottle again and brought it to the counter.

"How ya doin'?" the man said.

"Ugh. Work is grinding my ass," I groaned.

"Ditto, amigo."

I placed the bottle on the counter with a shaky hand. There was another customer hanging out next to the counter and he stared at my trembling hand.

"Why so shaky?" the other customer asked with a wink.

"'Cause this'll be my breakfast." I didn't even know where that came from. The customer nodded with an impressed frown.

"You know what suits me for that? I'll tell ya a secret formula for perfection. You know that stuff they give babies when they're dehydrated from diarrhea?"

"No," I said.

"Pedialyte," he answered. "Yeah. You take that and throw in a shot and a half of Everclear and hooo boy!"

"How come I never heard this?" the old man asked him.

"I'm not finished. You take that Pedialyte and mix it with that Everclear and then you top it off with some Mexican cough syrup. That's a drink."

"Jesus," the old man said. "You forgot the flaming rag stuffed in the bottleneck."

"Call it a 'Woman Tamer,'" the customer said.

"I could use three Woman Tamers right about now," I grumbled. "Two to drink and one to throw at my boss' house. Goddamn, I'm tired."

The guys nodded as the clerk rang me up.

"That'll be six-fifty."

"Donovan?"

Oh no.

The voice came from the liquor store entrance and was too familiar. It was one of my high school teachers, the cookie party one. Ms. K.

"Oh, hey."

"Are you selling this boy liquor?" she said to the old man. "I'm his teacher."

The man and his friend shook their heads as another bottle went under the counter.

Ms. K followed me into the parking lot.

"This isn't what I'd hope you'd be doing this summer."

"But it's not for me. It's for… someone else."

"Not a day goes by where I don't hear that one."

"I'm serious!"

"I think I should maybe go stop by The Roost and have a talk with your mother."

"Don't, I swear it's not for me!"

"Who is it for, then, Donovan?"

If I said it was for Dracula, it would just make things worse. Silence.

"That's what I thought. I don't want to see you trying to buy liquor or getting into trouble anymore—because I will, I *will* go to The Roost."

The emphasis she put on "will" let me know that the threat wasn't a bluff.

"Now get out of here," she said, nodding down the street. "Go play basketball, for God's sake."

I ran down the street, yeah, but to another liquor store. Castle Liquor. From the parking lot, I could hear heavy metal blasting inside. It felt like a good sign.

I walked in, grabbed the bottle, and approached the counter where a long-haired rocker stood behind the cash register.

"'Sup, bro!" the rocker said.

"Just this, please."

"Got i-dentity, man?"

"Oh, not on me. Do you take business cards?"

The rocker gave me a sympathetic smile and pointed above him.

"Sorry. Electric eye, bro. They just put it in last week. Some kid kept stealing beer."

I looked up and saw a camera pointed at me and immediately tensed up.

"Oh, don't worry, man. There's no audio. I just can't risk it. But, dude, check this out—I'll tell you how to do it. See that bum out there?"

He pointed past the parking lot to the corner where a bum was holding a cardboard sign that read THE MIDDLE IS HERE.

"Get him to go to the side of the store where cops can't see you and give him your order, tip him the change, and start fuckin' rockin'!" the metalhead said.

"Ohhh okay. Thanks."

I knew how this worked. I started to leave when the rocker called me back.

"Wait! Hey, is there some party going on tonight?" he asked.

"Huh?"

"The booze! Someone got a party goin' on?"

"Hmm, I don't know."

"Well, there'll be one now!" he yelled and broke into some wild-ass air guitar.

I walked around to the side of Castle Liquor and watched the crusty bum approach cars with his cardboard. The weather was good so most people's windows were down until the bum got close. I became less intimidated by him with each glass wall put up in his face. He took it in stride, but watching his hope rise and fall so often made me want to let him in on the food runner gig. That'd be weird though.

A green light made the bum retreat to the sidewalk where the sun beat down on him. He folded the cardboard over his head and shaded himself from the sun.

I flagged him over. The bum sprang to action faster than his appearance let on and he bolted across the street.

"Hey, hey, Joe, what'd ya know?" he said.

"How's it going?"

"It's going but it ain't gone, know what I mean?"

"What's up with that sign?"

The bum looked down to his cardboard.

"The middle, we're in it!"

"Huh?"

"Most guys like me have that 'end is near' shit going. I can't tell ya when that is—but until it happens, I can tell ya where the middle is!"

"Uh, hey, I'll give you the change from this if you can get me a fifth of Jack."

"At your service, milord," the bum said as he took the money with a bow. "Back in a flash!"

He disappeared around the corner while I leaned against the cool cinderblocks on the shady side of Castle Liquor. Relieved my mission was headed for success, I slid my butt to the ground and waited. And waited…

After twenty minutes had gone by, I started to think both the bum and the whiskey weren't coming back.

I'm fucked if I got scammed. Shit.

"Hey, hey!" The bum turned the corner waving a bottle in a tightly wrapped, brown paper bag. "Sorry I took so long. Since I was a 'paying customer,'" he said with a wink, "guy let me use the shitter. And I was carrying a heavy load, ya know? The AC in the back is amazing from the beer refrigeration too. Look! I've still got goosebumps." The sense of his true joy was tangible. It made me feel better about myself. This was working out.

"Anyways, here ya go." The bum handed me the bottle.

Now for real, this was the first time I had something regarded as contraband in my actual, true possession.

"Thanks for the tip, kid. Anytime you need me, I'm around."

I tucked the bottle under my shirt and walked back to the pier with a smile and the beginnings of a strut. I didn't want to make any money on this, I just wanted to be in with Dracula.

When I got back, I saw Renaldo balancing four nacho orders and two slush puppies in his arms.

"You got it? Told you."

"Yeah!" I said, flashing the bag.

"Better get your ass up there, man. He is pissed."

I walked up the ramp where Dracula was talking up a demonic nun and a zombie girl.

"There you are, Jesus!" he snarled.

"Hey." I thought this was going to go way better.

"You got the booze?"

"Yeah, here you go."

Dracula took the brown wrapper off the bottle.

"Oh, what the fuck?! Ancient Age? This is the cheapest fucking whiskey there is. I told you Drac drinks the Jack."

I didn't know what to say.

"You want me to go blind? Where are the rubs?"

I pulled the condoms out of my pocket and hoped for a better reaction.

"Un-lubricated?!?! You stupid fuck, these are going to rip my pubes out!"

"Uh, sorry."

"You're a shitty nacho bitch. Where's the change?"

"I don't have it."

"What? Don't try that shit on me. There should be plenty since you bought the world's crappiest everything."

"I had to give it to a bum to get the whiskey."

"Bullshit. Empty your pockets."

I fell under Dracula's command and pulled out the change I had made all afternoon.

"Yeah, that's what I thought, you liar."

Renaldo had been watching from a picnic table over.

"Leave him alone, he got you the stuff. That's his money from before."

"Shut up, you beaner. I'll get you banned from here so quick you'll have to go pick strawberries."

Renaldo fumed and held his anger in. It was true, Dracula had the most pull at the Castle.

"Come on, lighten up," the zombie girl said.

"Fuck that." And he snatched the money out of my hand.

I stood there as Dracula disappeared into the Castle.

"That sucked," Renaldo said under his breath.

I turned around and faced a bunch of cast members watching behind me. The dudes turned their backs but a couple chicks took pity on me. The demonic nun and zombie girl came over. They were both hot as monsters but the demonic nun was totally incredible. I couldn't imagine what was underneath the getup, but what was on top totally worked. Seeing her walk in my direction, actually toward me, was a new rush.

"Hey, don't worry about it, he's a dick anyways," the zombie girl said. "He's acting that way because you're taller than him."

"Yeah?" Thanks, Zombie Girl, but I really want to know what the demonic nun has to say.

"Why do you think he likes being on the mantel so much?"

"Oh." Okay, Zombie Girl was cool.

"What's your name?" the demonic nun said.

"Donovan." Success! She speaks!

"You need a real job. I know the manager is looking to hire someone, want me to introduce you to him?"

"That'd be really cool."

They went to get the manager. Renaldo got up and elbowed me.

"Dude, are you sure you want to give up what we've got going here?" he asked.

"Dude, yeah!"

Renaldo looked disappointed.

"Our own hours? Our own boss? Our own money?"

"What money?" I said, pulling my pockets out.

"Fuck, man."

The Castle's back door opened and a short, fat man in his forties came out smoking a cigar, wearing a Hawaiian shirt and corduroy shorts. The mostly unbuttoned shirt showed off his extensive bed of chest hair, so thick that his gold chain just floated on top of it.

"You the kid?"

"Uh, I dunno." This was happening fast.

"You're the fuckin' kid. How old are you?"

"Six—"

The guy shook his head before I could finish.

"Sev—?"

He shook his head again.

"Eighteen?" I said.

"Ha, whatever. So you want a job here?"

"Yeah!"

"Four bucks an hour, under the table."

I was confused.

"You get paid, you just don't get a pay slip."

"No problem."

"Be here tomorrow, ten o'clock."

"Thank you so much, this is like a dream come true."

"What's your name?"

"Donovan."

"Donovan, welcome to my fuckin' nightmare. I'm Jack Spires."

He threw the cigar down and went back inside. The open door let out all kinds of screams coming from inside the Castle.

Renaldo got up from the table.

"Dude, so you're just gonna ditch me now, huh?" he said.

"No way. But fuck, man. The Castle!"

"Alright, bro. I get it. But don't get all weird on me when you're a big shot. Or I'll spit in your nachos."

"I promise I won't get weirder than I already am."

"Okay, then we'll make a plan to punch Dracula in the fucking face on Saturday."

The next morning, I showed up an hour early to the Castle. The pier was empty and I used the time to walk around every inch of it, now that I would be "Donovan… from the Castle." I went to the end of the pier and looked out at the ocean, the horizon, and breathed in the salty air. But it didn't matter how picturesque it was. I turned my back to it and gazed down the pier toward the Castle. My heart beat with anticipation and intimidation.

Just before ten o'clock, as the steel gates rolled up on the arcade, food stands, and carnival games, I walked to the back door, eager to get inside the Castle. I joined the group of about forty people gathered by the back door. A community of individuals, all dressed in street clothes and without makeup yet, ranged in age from older teens and early twenties to a few in their thirties. They were all older, confident, relaxed, cooler—just more of everything I wanted to be. Most of the people looked far too normal to be concerned with the dark side. The Castle was their frat house. But a small group of the older ones did not hang around for the same reason. They were social rejects you'd cross the street to avoid. If they were prone to talking to themselves and threatening the skies while off the clock, they would certainly be an authentic fit for the Castle. No acting required. I was too nervous to talk to any of them and stared at the backs of their heads and sides of their faces.

I stopped scanning the group when I came to this one girl. She was uniquely perfect. Her incredible combination of bright blue eyes and a glowing round face pushed my heart into my throat. If I wasn't so fascinated by her face, I would have noticed her hair first. It was feathered and dyed completely green, totally rare around Dunes. The green hair was an awesome invitation. It was like a flashing OPEN TO WEIRDOS LIKE YOU sign on her head. I must have stared too long because she noticed and turned toward me.

"Hey, you're here!" she said, scaring the shit out of me.

It was a familiar voice, a scratchy coastal drawl that made you want to hear her talk about anything. I couldn't remember ever talking to a chick that hot, minus that demonic nun from yesterday. Who I still wasn't sure had even been real.

"Uh, hey?" I coughed up.

"It's me!"

"Sorry?"

"From yesterday. The nun? I'm Melody."

"Oh! Hey! I'm Donovan."

I had never seen a girl look so beautiful as both a human and a member of the dark side. Good or evil, I'd take both.

"Did Jack get you a job?"

"Yeah! Fucking thanks!"

"Awesome. Well, hopefully we get to do a room together soon!"

A week ago, I couldn't imagine working in the Castle or a hot chick talking to me without sneering, and now both are happening.

"Yeah, totally," I said.

"You're tall enough to be Executioner, maybe you'll get to slay me!"

"I would totally slay you," I said while trying to process what she meant by "slay" and that she even used the word "slay."

Melody laughed at my vow.

Jack came out through the back door and banged his clipboard on the front table to get everyone's attention.

"Anyways, good luck!" she said and joined her group of friends while I was still lost in over-excited thought. Every day before this one sucked…

Jack coughed and addressed the group.

"Alright, it's gonna be the first real big one of the summer so I hope you're all ready for the kingdom of madness. And I don't mean in a cool way. Don't take shit from anybody tonight."

This sounded both awesome and profoundly inspirational.

"We've got RJ on Rat Room. Beth in Nightmare Tavern. Bobby in the Graveyard. Blake, you're a roaming zombie. TJ, you are… Executioner… with Melody."

Whoever TJ is, he sucks and is slaying the queen of my dreams.

One by one, everyone's name was called as they went inside to apply their assigned makeup and costumes.

Jack looked up from his clipboard and saw only me left.

"Ah, yeah, new kid! Ready?"

"Yeah!"

"Come with me."

We walked down the pier, away from the Castle. I had so many questions I wanted to ask.

"So is, like, that hearse yours?" was the best I could think of in the moment.

"Yeah, don't hold it against me," Jack said.

"What? No. It's awesome."

"Ha! Yeah, strip clubs make me park it a block away."

I was confused. Was he taking such a sweet car for granted? But it wasn't important. The real question was Why are we walking away from the Castle?

"Isn't the Castle back there?" I said.

"Sure is!"

Jack didn't really pay attention to me. He was busy saying "hey" to people who knew him on the pier. He called the girls "doll" and the guys he liked "mack." I wanted to be a "mack" and not "the kid." Jack pretended to be a tough asshole and maybe he was, but I sensed there was another side to him.

We came upon the food vendor section that I already knew so well. Behind the counter sat Tony, a devoted and miserable man, feeding the Castle Pizza carousel with pepperoni slices.

"Tony, this is…"

"We know each other from food runs," I said as Tony nodded.

"Great. So he's gonna work with you from now on."

Now on?

"I could use it," Tony said.

"He'd be perfect for the pizza guitar," Jack said.

"Yeah." Tony nodded.

Pizza guitar? My dream took a nosedive.

"Let's move some 'za, boys!" Jack slapped me on the back and left.

Fuck. I wanted a job on the front of the Castle Dunes brochure, not on the back of it.

"No more running back and forth, huh? Welcome aboard," Tony said.

I watched Jack disappear down the pier as I stood frozen, paralyzed from shock.

"Here ya go," Tony said, handing me a heavy metal–styled cardboard guitar with promotional pizza graphics on it that read "Hot 'n Ready!"

I grabbed the cardboard guitar and looked at it as I took my first breath in a while. Was Renaldo right?

"What am I supposed to do with this?" I asked.

"Your job is to play this thing in front of here, and try to wrangle people over to buy a slice."

I thought I said something to acknowledge the instructions but nothing came out.

"What's that?" Tony asked.

"Okay, yeah. Yes."

"Think you can handle it?" Tony raised an eyebrow.

"Totally."

"At lunch I'll give you a coke and two slices if you're doing good."

"Cool."

"Alright then, get at it," Tony said.

There wasn't anyone even on the pier yet. Just me, the pizza guitar, and the rising temperature. I wanted to terrify people in the darkness, not get laughed at in the sun.

I began trying out a variety of grips on the guitar, looking for one that felt right. There were none. I stood there with my knees locked, mock strumming as I stared at my shoes. A couple walked by, not paying attention to me. I was horrified anyways and turned my back to them and stared at Tony.

"Kid, don't sell me the fucking pizza. Sell them!"

"Okay."

"And you also need to be yelling 'Hot 'n Ready!' in a heavy metal voice," Tony said.

"Are you fucking with me?"

"Ya know, if you're too shy for this, we can get someone else."

"No, no. I got it."

I walked out to the middle of the pier, strumming the guitar high up on my chest, and worked up the courage to say, "Hot 'n Ready," at a decent volume.

No one paid attention to me. Thankfully, my pizza song fell on deaf ears.

I turned my performance toward the Castle. So close, yet so… disappointing. But I guess as long as I was within a stone's throw, it beat anything else. As I gazed at the Castle, I got caught up in my thoughts and stopped pizza rocking.

"Kid! Hot 'n Ready! Hot 'n Ready! Hot 'n fucking Ready!"

"Yeah, sorry."

"I've got enough shit to worry about, alright?"

The pier had started to fill up and I let one rip, "Hoooot 'nnnnnn Reaaaa-daaaay!" My voice cracked halfway through "ready" and made everyone within fifty feet laugh out loud. Families with their kids, bored teenagers, couples looking for something to do. Now my awkwardness was the attraction.

My cheeks filled with icy blood. I looked to Tony for help.

"Don't look to me for a sign, kid. You're holding it."

I resumed wandering a small perimeter around Castle Pizza, trying my best to yell "Hot 'n Ready!" every thirty seconds with just a passable amount of panache. All while constantly strumming guitar like a man with two broken hands.

"D!"

It was Renaldo.

"Ha ha, shredding some cheese! You're the new Hot 'n Ready guy, huh? That's cool… I guess."

"Kinda," I said, trying to maintain my silent song.

Renaldo took a step back.

"Dude, don't you watch music videos? That's not how you play that shit!" he said.

Tony yelled from behind the counter, "Renaldo, show 'em how it's done and I'll give you a slice."

"I'll show him but your pizza sucks, dude. Give me free refills all day and I'll turn Donovan into a shredder."

"Deal. And fuck you."

"You play guitar?" I asked.

"Nah, but it's not about that. Okay, first off, you're playing that shit way too high. Only assholes do that. You gotta hold it down low. You want to be strumming your dick. That's where the action is. Playing guitar is pure cocksmanship."

I tried it out.

"Alright. But don't hold your picking hand like that, take your thumb and index finger and put them together while you fan out the rest of the fingers."

"I don't get it," I said.

"Like you're making an "OK" sign but pinch your fingers together."

I did what he said.

"Yeah, man. Alright, now the other hand. You can't just stay in one spot like that on the neck. That would be the most boring fucking song you'd ever hear. You gotta go all over, man, that's the shred."

I went up and down the neck like I was wiping it off.

"No. Arch your fingers more. Like spider legs. Yeah, bro, now do it all together."

I began to pick it up.

"Hey, Tony," Renaldo yelled. "I want a half Coke, quarter 7up, half Dr Pepper, and the rest Cactus Cooler soda," Renaldo yelled.

"You skipped too many math classes. I'm not pouring that shit all day."

"Check it out, though. Donovan, shred, dude."

I pointed a ripping solo and heavy metal frown at Tony.

"Ha! Not bad! You're a natural, Dono."

I didn't want to be a natural at cardboard pizza guitar.

"Keep yelling, though," Tony said, nodding to the pizza. "This shit's been on the rack for, like, two days."

It didn't matter to me how old the pizza was or that I properly played the cardboard guitar. It couldn't have been any less Castle-y. Wait, no. The Roost was less Castle-y. When based on distance away from Janice and proximity to the Castle, pizza was the clear winner. And I kept reminding myself.

Renaldo leaned up against the railing opposite the pizza and watched me relaunch into advertising.

"Hot 'n Ready!" I yelled.

I found a groove with Tony and Renaldo's approval and widened my perimeter a little as the pier started to fill up that afternoon. Some girls walked past me a few times, giggling, and I could never figure out if it was the good or bad kind.

Jack walked past me in the thick of the afternoon and gave me an approving nod. I still felt suckered.

Renaldo stepped in.

"Dude, you've got some hot licks down now but you're boring me to death. You need some moves, man!"

"Like what?"

"Like shake it up, bro. Do a sprinkler head."

"What's that?"

"Dude!"

Renaldo air guitared as he swept the tip of the guitar across a

180-degree angle, then reset from the beginning to start the 180 over at the same spot.

"It's like the tip of your guitar is spraying the arena with fucking metal power."

"I'll try it."

"Dude, you don't 'try' this shit—you fuckin' fuck it. Get out there and spray them down!"

I attempted my first sprinkler head move. But went from left to right and right to left in a smooth direction.

"No, no, no."

"What?"

"Dude, that looks weak."

"But this is what you said."

"You gotta do it like a sprinkler. Reset back to the beginning when you get to the end. No back and forth."

"What's the difference?"

"The difference is rad versus fucking lame."

"Dude, are you fucking with me?"

"Hey, you wanted it, suit yourself," Renaldo shrugged. "If you need me, I'll be under the pier smoking weed with my boss."

"Who?"

"Exactly."

He disappeared in the crowd and I returned to my pizza guitar.

"Hot 'n Ready!" I cried out.

I played that cardboard guitar into the night, 'til my fingers bled, like they say in rock songs. Only these were paper cuts. Finally, Tony called the day and told me to eat. I sat down behind the Castle Pizza counter and had a slice. Tony squinted at me.

"Whoa, buddy. Did you put any sunscreen on today? You look like a lobster."

I went to check my reflection in the mirror. My pale skin had turned bright red and I suddenly began to feel my face throb. I was supposed to be inside the Castle and hadn't thought of sunscreen the whole day. I'd gotten too occupied with embarrassment and pizza guitar techniques.

"I've never been this sunburned in my life! What am I gonna do tomorrow?"

"Wear sunscreen I hope, ha!"

"Seriously, Tony."

"I don't know, but this pizza sure as shit doesn't sell itself."

The next morning, I passed the screams coming from the Castle and shuffled in sunburned pain down the pier to Castle Pizza.

Tony erupted in laughter when he saw me.

"Holy shit, kid! You look like a cartoon character that got angry."

"Yeah, maybe I should do something else today?"

"Nah. I'll set up the picnic parasol and you'll be good."

"I don't know if I can move a lot."

"Oh, don't worry about that, it's attention we want and that face is gonna get it."

I stood in place, hardly opening my mouth as people repeatedly came by to make comments.

I spotted Todd, one of the jock assholes from high school, and then he saw me. I clutched my cardboard guitar and looked away.

"Hot 'n Ready," I muttered.

Just then, Todd clipped me with his shoulder.

"What the fuck!" he said, acting like it was my fault. "Hey, guys, check it out. The Prince of Dorkness."

"Yeah! Look at that fucking dork!" said another jock as Todd pushed me into the sun.

"Ow!"

"Holy shit, you are fucking burned," Todd said, grabbing my arm. "That feel good?"

I collapsed under the grip.

"You guys, come on. I'm working."

"A fucking pizza guitar?" Todd said while giving it a punch.

"Come on, guys. Please."

Tony interrupted the scene.

"Donovan, stop socializing and sell some fucking pizza." Tony's attention went back to filling orders.

"Just leave me alone, seriously."

"Or what?"

"Yeah! Or what?" the other jock said.

"Hot 'n Ready! Hot 'n Ready!!" It seemed like a good defense in the moment. This time, I hoped drawing attention to myself would keep me out of trouble.

"This fuckin' guy. You gave my girlfriend nightmares for weeks with that shit you pulled at the talent show."

I couldn't help but smile.

"You think that's funny?"

"Uh…"

Tony butted in. "Donovan, if I have to tell you one more time!"

"Hotnreadyhotnreadyhotnready!" Why didn't Tony know this was code for "Help!"?

I scurried out from the shade, away from the jocks and into the sun. It burned and made me think of Dracula's famous sensitivity to daylight.

"Where do you think you're going?"

"Dude, seriously. I'm fucking working." Maybe a little bark back would get me out of this. It didn't.

"Oh, that's it. Boys, let's show him how to surf."

I might have been taller, but these guys' low gravity was dangerous for my stilt-like legs.

The jocks all grabbed me and tossed me off the pier while passersby just laughed. Whose side should they have been on? The letterman jackets, or the sunburned freak, playing a cardboard pizza guitar? Tony was too busy to cast a vote.

The jocks looked down on me as I plummeted. They high-fived and yelled, "Shoot the pier, bro! Hahahaha!"

I hit the water with the pizza guitar still in hand. I thought my skin was going to melt off from the pain of the water contact. If it had been low tide, I would have broken my neck. Instead, I was swept among the barnacle-covered pillars holding up the pier. Above me, clusters of sleeping bats covered the bottom of the pier.

The waves continued to push me against the pillars. One finally got me good across my arm when I braced myself for the blow. The only thing more painful than an extreme sunburn was a gash across it with saltwater pouring in.

After what seemed like eternity in tumult lost at sea, I crawled onto the shore, dripping blood and tangled in seaweed.

"Holy shit, bro!" It was Renaldo, running toward me from his usual post at the bottom of the employee ramp. "That was badass! I've never had the balls to jump off the pier."

Renaldo saw my arm.

"Oh fuck, the pier took a bite out of you. Damn."

I tried to catch my breath.

"Dude, you're hero of the day, man," he said.

"They… threw… me… off," I managed to say.

"Fuckin' who?"

"Jocks."

"Fucking jocks, man! The same ones from…"

I shook my head.

"Jesus, they're everywhere. Dude, we gotta stop that bleeding."

Renaldo tore the centerpiece heavy metal patch off the back of his jacket.

"Here, dude. Hold this over it."

Renaldo wrapped the patch around the wound and squeezed.

"Owww!"

"I know, bro. But this'll have to do."

I looked down at the patch. It was for a singer named King and featured a medieval knight battling a dragon.

"Hold that tight."

"I gotta go back to work."

"Dude, you're a mess. Fuck it."

"No, I gotta."

"Dude, your arm looks like a slice of pizza, and your face is fucked," Renaldo said.

"Thanks, man. Seriously."

I dripped my way back to Castle Pizza.

"Where the hell have you been? Why are you all wet? You're not getting paid to fuckin' swim," Tony said.

"I got thrown off."

Tony paused, closed his eyes, and nodded.

"Shit, kid. I'm sorry. It happens, ya know?"

No. I didn't know.

"Where's the guitar?"

"The ocean."

"Shit. No offense, but you're more replaceable than the pizza guitar."

"None taken. It was true art."

"So it's a good thing we've got this," Tony said and pulled out a cardboard pizza saxophone.

I was crushed. Now everyone walking by got a good laugh at the bleeding, wet kid blowing on a pizza sax. Everyone. It made me realize guitars are cooler than I thought.

Finally, Jack walked up.

"How's it goin' here?" he asked Tony.

"Not too good, look at the kid."

"Damn. You got thrown off, huh?"

"Yeah."

"I'm surprised the lobsters didn't take you in as one of their own."

Tony and Jack laughed. I could have used some sympathy. I was used to not getting any, but I'd hoped that could change.

"I hit the pier."

I tried to peel back part of the patch covering the wound but it had already bonded to my flesh.

"Gross, kid. You should go home and take care of that."

"No, I want to work."

Jack raised an eyebrow and nodded at me.

"What do you want to do? Can't sell food with a gaper like that."

"I got customers," Tony said and ducked out.

"I want to work in the Castle, people are crazy out here on the pier," I told Jack.

"The Castle, huh. Well, are you crazy?"

"I don't think so."

"Kid, I'm crazy. That's why I'm here. So you must be crazy, too."

"I promise I'll be good in there."

Jack squinted.

"It'll cost you."

"How much? I don't have any money really."

"Price of admission is your mind."

"Please take it away from me. I don't need it."

"Okay, kid. I'll give you a Castle job, but it's no safer in there than out here. It's worse."

"I can take it."

"And it's not going to be what you think. It's a lot bigger drop from up there," he said, pointing up at the Castle.

"Just please give me a shot."

"Alright. I will. But it's not 'cause you don't need makeup to look like a weirdo," Jack said, laughing.

"I'm good with that."

"Don't say I didn't warn you. And if anyone asks, tell 'em you're eighteen."

5

Jack led me past the ghosts and ghouls smoking cigarettes in back of the Castle. The dude who played Satan stopped me.

"Hey, can I get two slices?" he said in full makeup.

"He's busy," Jack said.

That's right I'm fucking busy. I ignored him and followed the real boss of monsters.

Jack opened the Castle door and held it for me.

"Bet ya didn't know Hell had a back door, huh? Leave it to me to make one!" Jack said as he backslapped me into the Castle. A blast of trapped heat escaped out the door as a variety of customers' screams could be heard a few thin walls away.

"I hope you like it hot, Dono!"

Dono? Jack said it with ease, as though it had been my long-standing nickname. I couldn't remember anyone giving me another name that wasn't an insult.

Jack took me down a dimly lit corridor. It wasn't painted with bloody stone like the rest of the Castle I had seen. Instead, raw sheets of water-stained plywood were held in place by casually hammered nails. Local rock show and keg party flyers peeled off the walls. Wiring for the occasional light bulb was exposed along the ceiling and flickered every time a decent-sized wave hit the pier columns below. When I went through the castle as a plebe, I thought the dimming was part of the effect.

We entered the makeup room, a low-ceilinged plywood room covered in graffiti, jokes about staff members, fake epitaphs, and heavy metal logos. Jack tossed me a dark-brown druid robe, the same that I had seen so many in the Castle wear.

"Here's your uniform. Keep this on the whole time you're here so everyone knows you're a part of the Castle and not some punk."

"A part of the Castle..." The phrase echoed in my head. It was really happening. An outsider on the inside.

"Normally, you're supposed to wear some black around your eyes and fill in the rest with white, but that sunburn looks scarier than anything in here," Jack said with a laugh as big as his gut.

Oh, yeah, the sunburn. I was too pumped to remember how much pain I was in.

"I can handle it," I said and threw the robe on. It was itchy and had a built-in stench of sweat, smoke, and beer.

Jack pointed to the makeup table. Eight chairs sat in front of a wide mirror with light bulbs lining it.

"Help yourself. Everyone does their own makeup."

I stepped up to the table and dug two fingers into a tin of Pure Black and circled my eyes. While I was working it in, Jack broke down the Castle's ins and outs.

"Couple things to know about working here," he said, pulling up a chair and a drink. "Show up on time. If you're sick, come to work. If you're really sick, call me. Don't fuck off too much, I'm not an idiot. I know what goes on here but just don't take it too far."

I wanted to ask, "What really does go on here?" but pretended to know what he was talking about.

"Also, you have to stay within the Castle walls and the break area right out back. No walking the pier in costume. You know the deal there. And I'm surprised how important I need to make this next one but some people... if you see any mushrooms in the Castle, do not eat them. They're not the trippy kind. They'll make you see God, you just won't be coming back!" Jack let out another laugh. "But seriously. Don't eat that shit."

"Got it," I said, reaching for the tin of Clown White face paint, smearing it around the rest of my face.

"Also, as you might have noticed, this place has seen better days. It's not the monsters that'll kill you here—it's the building. If you're not careful, it's a death trap. Flights of stairs in dark, confusing twists and turns," he said as the lights flickered. "The electrical. Everything."

I finished the makeup by adding a couple touches of black to make a downturned mouth. I looked in the mirror and smiled as much as the makeup was frowning.

"Great job, here's your mop," Jack said, handing it over.

"A mop? Shouldn't I have a scythe or, like, an axe?"

"You're the new Castle custodian, Dono."

"Wait, what?"

"You wanted a job in the Castle, right?"

"Yeah."

"Well…"

"No, I'm in. I just thought—" I said when Jack cut me off.

"Here's your walkie-talkie. Strap it on your pants under your robe. Now, there are multiple codes we use to discreetly identify situations that need attention. It's your job to respond to some of these codes."

"Codes?" Yeah, codes? Walkie-talkies? Mops? How is any of this spooky?

"Codes, Dono. Still up for this?"

"Yeah, totally." It was more true than not.

Jack went through all the various codes to know. Codes for hurt cast members, hurt customers, overly scared customers, and more.

"Cast members get hurt?" I asked.

"Oh, yeah, a lot of people's reaction to a good scare is a punch in the face. Sometimes more."

"What do I do?"

"I'll take care of that. Just stay on your toes. But the next codes apply to you more directly than others."

"Okay."

"They're easy to remember. There's Code Yellow, Green, and Brown. Code Yellow, this happens multiple times a day. Someone pissed in the Castle. The plebes are drunk and stuck in a forty-five-minute maze so they just piss in any dark corner. If there's carpet, throw the cleaner down. If it's not carpet, use the mop."

Jack picked up a plastic Castle Dunes cup, took a slug, and let out a "Woo!"

"Now Code Green, that's puke. Same people. Do about the same thing. Then there's Code Brown." Jack sighed. "Bummer, but it happens."

"Like, people shit in the Castle?"

"There's so many dark areas in the Castle, you can't imagine what people do. A Brown? Two reasons. One, the food on the pier. Man, it's gotten me a couple times."

Jack took another swig.

"And two, you've heard the expression 'scared shitless'?"

"Yeah."

"It's not just an expression. And if you shit your pants, you aren't going to take them off in a horror maze. No, you're going to shit-limp all the way out, leaving a trail that tumbled out your pant leg. Follow the trail."

"Follow the trail."

"You got it. There's one last one, Code Gold."

"Gold?"

"That means go behind Dracula's mantel, where he waits to appear in the main room. He sits on the other side of that portrait all day, waiting for groups to enter. He's the longest-running cast member. You might have seen him in the commercials."

"Oh yeah."

"Have you met him yet?"

"Kinda."

"He's an asshole, huh?"

I didn't know how to respond.

"Well, he's the star of this place. People love it when they see the same guy from the commercials, and as a result, he gets some special considerations. Like Code Gold."

"Sounds cool."

"It means, go get the bucket from him and empty it out."

"What's in the bucket?"

"Pee."

"Why does he pee in a bucket?"

"It's the only post in the whole Castle that cannot be abandoned. He brings you into the whole experience, sets the tone. No one cares if the Haunted Forest is vacant. But you can't drop the ball at tip-off so he's… important. But to answer your question, I have no goddamn idea."

I thought I was graduating from the pizza guitar to something more. Not cleaning and removing bodily fluids from the Castle. But, fuck it, it was still the Castle and that was enough.

"Code Gold, empty the bucket. Gotcha."

"He might make other requests but those are up to your own discretion."

I let out a puff of air through my nose and nodded.

"Stay on channel one on the walkie. When you're not responding to codes, I want you roaming between the walls, the storage rooms, anything considered backstage. Look for dead rats. There's traps all over. If you see a dead one, throw it in your sack, reset it, and put another piece of cheese down."

"Like real rats?"

"Hell yeah, real ones. This place has got more real rats than fake ones."

One of the most unforgettable rooms in the Castle involved rats both fake and real. You walked into the room and stepped across a plexiglass floor that was crawling with real rats under it. Then the room goes dark and you feel rats on your feet and legs but those are the fake ones. Jack told me that the problem began when the rats once chewed through their contained area and multiplied in legion. This worked for the Castle most of the time—customers were horrified at the "realistic" props. But it really grossed everyone out who worked there and knew, and was surrounded by, the truth.

"Gotta clean 'em up or this place starts reeking death. And I mean that in a bad way," Jack said.

A group of screams erupted a wall away. I processed my shrouded custodial duties by thinking I would be the most terrifying character in the whole place. Who else would smell like bleach and have a sack of dead rats over their shoulder?

"If you get lost, any hallway will get you where you're going, it just might take a while. Dig it?"

"Thanks, Jack, seriously."

Jack slapped me on the back again.

"Thank me later if you still want to. Now get to work."

In the employee passageways between the rooms, there was a rat trap every ten feet. Each one was occupied. I quickly developed a routine of using a pooper-scooper and my foot to release each rat and toss it into the bag. Then I'd spring the trap back and lay down some American cheese. I was at it for so long that the cheese started looking good.

While creeping the interior walls, I came across one of the spooky red windows everyone sees. Seen from the other side, they weren't spooky at all. It was just some red plastic that was held up with rusty staples. A light bulb in the center of it mimicked a candle. These were all over the Castle. I stared through the murky red window while screams and laughter passed through the room on the other side.

It was the Dungeon room, a set piece–centered room where mannequins tortured one another. To add a scare to the room, a zombie dude hid near the red window, jumping out at people who thought the room was empty. It looked like a dream job. I stood there and watched for twenty minutes. The rats weren't getting any deader.

When the plebes trickled down to nothing, the zombie became restless and pulled a joint out and lit it up. I couldn't let this first day in the Castle go by without scaring someone. I had to get in on the action. I saw the rush and wanted to be a part of it. The zombie took his deepest hit yet and admired the joint while he held the smoke in. Through the red window, I could see his eyes water as he held it down with a snorty grunt.

"Boo!" I yelled and slammed my flashlight against the plywood wall at the same time. The zombie choked on his packed lungs and let out a shrill, high-pitched scream while smoke shot out of his mouth. He doubled over, still trying to clear his lungs.

"Who the fuck is that?"

I crouched down and didn't make a sound.

"Who fucking is that? Goddamn it, I'm trying to work," he said while putting out the joint.

I snuck down the hallway, victorious, and went back to the traps. The work was tedious but even between the walls, the atmosphere was endlessly entertaining. If I could get one scare in like that every day, I'd be fulfilled living with vermin.

No codes were called on the walkie until night came.

"Code Green, Mirror of Death."

Someone had actually barfed on the Mirror itself. I went in the identical room on the backside of the Mirror. The skeleton guy was crouched below the Mirror.

"Hey, so, yeah. Some dude actually puked on the Mirror," he said in weary disbelief.

"Okay."

"Isn't that fucked up? I pop up to scare him and he's just cross-eyed and blows chunks. I scared the shit out of him, though."

I laughed.

"Yeah, well have at it."

I walked around and pulled the cleaner bottle off my hip. The Mirror was wet and dripping yellow bile down the wall and to the floor. I squirted the cleaner all over and began wiping the area down. There were bits of pizza mixed in, with the teeth marks still clearly visible. I thought I was done with Castle Pizza but it was coming back to haunt me, as if striking from the grave. The room's audio started up on its usual loop and spoke a different oracle than the one I'd heard when first going through the Castle as a plebe.

"Gaze into the Mirror of Death," it said at the start of each loop. I reapplied the cleaner to the Mirror as it told me about "a death in the family" and its "profound lesson." I didn't know anyone that died. Ever. Another one came on after it, telling me, "There's a love interest in your life." Now we're talking. I listened to the Mirror's advice: "Go and find that person in the halls of Castle Dunes."

"Code... Gold..." the walkie said in Dracula's terrible Transylvanian accent.

I hurried over behind Dracula's mantel and hoped I could redeem myself with him. Maybe demonstrating proper waste management would change his mind about me.

Dracula sat on a chair, reading a porno mag with his legs up on a two-by-four that was nailed to the plywood wall. His black dress shoes had lifts on them. He was even shorter than I'd thought. The room was almost the size of a closet. The raw walls were covered with water stains and little score-keeping check marks by Dracula's head.

"You?" Dracula said. "What the fuck are you doing here?"

"I'm the new Castle custodian."

"Pffft, you don't deserve to be here. Where did you study?"

"Dunes High."

"I mean acting, you dipshit."

"I didn't. I've watched a lot of horror movies though."

"I've elevated this role beyond stupid horror."

I wanted to ask if his lifts were part of the elevation process.

"I'm just here to get the bucket, man."

"That's right, you are. I suppose I'll let you carry my piss."

A red bulb in the ceiling flashed on and off.

"Get the fuck out of here, I'm on."

Dracula got into position as thunder blasted from the other side of the wall. I grabbed the bucket and left.

At the end of the night, I went back to the makeup table to remove my face paint with the others. Melody was there, wiping away her demonic face. She looked up into the mirror and saw me.

"Hey!" she said, turning around and extending a hug.

I stalled in disbelief.

"I smell really bad, I don't know if you want to get close," I said.

"So do I!" she said, laughing as she pressed her body against mine. I had to stick my butt out so I didn't poke her.

"How's it going? Are you stoked to be here?" she said.

"Yeah... it's awesome."

"What do they have you doing?"

"Uh, cleaning stuff."

"Oh, damn, well, maybe they'll see how great you are and promote you out of that soon."

The word "great" made me freeze up. I was more used to taking insults than compliments. I just stared at her.

"Anyways… a few of us are going to Brogi's after. Wanna join?"

Brogi's was the local dive bar, populated by old drunks during the day who relinquished it to the younger ones at night. Definitely lofty, forbidden ground for a sixteen year old. I didn't have a fake ID and even if I did, I didn't have the money. But I wasn't going to admit to either.

"That's cool. I, uh, wore my pants that don't have pockets today so I, uh, don't have my wad with me."

I couldn't look her straight in the eye so I deflected to the next thing that drew my attention—her tits. She caught me in the act immediately.

"You're funny. But if you change your mind, I'll be there. Okay, wad pockets?"

"Alrighty," I said. I had never used the word "alrighty" in my life. Why did it have to happen now?

Melody laughed nonchalantly and took off.

"Dude!" I found Renaldo under the pier smoking a J with his headphones on loud enough to hear ten feet away. I approached him from behind and tapped him on the shoulder. Renaldo jumped back and fell into a ready-for-anything stance.

"Jesus, dude. I was this close to killing you," he said.

"Sorry, man."

"I can do it, you know. Death blow. Learned it from a guy who lived on the beach last year."

"Okay, what is it, then?"

"Well, if I showed you, you'd die."

"Dude, anyways, do you want to hear about my day in there or what?"

"Sure, what's the ratio like?" Renaldo said.

"The ratio?"

"Chicks versus dudes. The ratio."

"There's this one chick…"

"That's all it takes, bro!"

"Yeah?"

"Oh, yeah. Big titties?"

"Actually, I think so." That's not the reason I was attracted to Melody, but I wasn't going to turn them down.

"Go on."

"I've only seen her with one of those Castle robes on but there's a pretty serious shelf going on," I said, motioning around my chest.

"A shelf!"

"Yeah. She caught me staring at it."

"Uh oh, what'd she say?"

"She said, 'You're funny.'"

"Oh, shiiiit."

"What's that mean?"

"Dude, it doesn't mean you're funny. It means come and suck on these motherfuckers!"

"Really?"

"Trust me."

"Whoa."

"So did you bang her on break?"

"Uh, no."

The "Toccata" coming from the front of the Castle finally shut off for the night.

"There's always tomorrow," Renaldo said.

I walked home from the Castle. As I passed the Odd Fellows Cemetery, my head was still spinning and replaying glimpses of the Castle in action. The crouched monsters. The busty witches. Satanic altars. Even though I was cleaning puke, I had never been filled with such a sense of triumph and belonging. I inhaled the night air and scanned the cemetery. It looked different now. Pointless. Before all this, I was a hopeless freak. Or if I was being nice to myself, I'd say "brooding loner." But before this, the me-without-a-Castle era, I was vulnerable to attack. People wanted an explanation as to why I was weird. Now I had one. I was no longer "Donovan from the cemetery" or "Donovan from the pizza place." I was finally "Donovan from the Castle." The Castle! I carried its walls home with me.

I snuck through the window to avoid Janice. But when I got in my room, I saw the hallway light turn off under the crack of my door. She knew I was home and did a good job of pretending not to care. Maybe she didn't.

I woke up super early and got to the Castle before anyone. The "Toccata" wasn't even playing yet. All the games, food stands, and arcade doors were closed. It felt different being around the pier now—my new sense of purpose replaced years of loitering and longing.

Jack arrived and started throwing switches, turning on the music. He asked me to walk through the Castle with him on "inspection detail," which meant me picking up trash and finding unattended codes. Getting to walk the Castle without any plebes inside confirmed the fact that I really did want to live there. When we came across the Funeral Parlor room, I found out we weren't alone. Apparently I wasn't the only one who thought it'd be a cool place to live.

Melody was asleep in an open coffin. Jack wasn't pleased.

"Sweetie, wake up," Jack said.

Melody opened her eyes. She was a beautiful vagrant.

"Oh, hey… shit," she said with a sticky, dry mouth.

"You can't sleep here, doll. This is your first offense so I'll let it slide."

"Thanks, Jack."

"If you need some help, we'll find some."

"No, it's not like that. My parents think I'm at camp."

"Let's ask around today, we'll find you somewhere safe."

"It's cool." She didn't seem to care where she ended up by the end of the day. I wanted to volunteer my face as a place to stay.

"Hey," she said to me.

"Good morning, or should I say good mourrrning?" I said, immediately regretting it as she yawned a courtesy smile.

Jack's eyes darted between us, and he shook his head at me.

"Let's keep it moving," he said and we continued inspection detail, now with Melody.

"Gonna be one of those hot ones today. Hope you guys are ready," Jack said.

"I'm ready," Melody said, privately winking at me. She had woken up pretty fast.

"Uh, I'm ready too," I said and squinted both eyes by mistake.

When we got up to the Castle roof outside, I asked Jack if it would be cool if I stayed up there for a little while.

"Are you gonna jump off?" he asked.

"No!"

"Sure. Best view in town, right? I should have a restaurant up here! See ya at roll call."

"Later, Donovan," Melody said. I loved hearing her say my name. It wasn't full of the normal tone of disgust I usually heard. She said it like there was something she liked about me. It made me like myself too.

I took in the view and thought about my new position. I was

somebody. I never got a gold star in school, but now I had a pentagram to my name. I thought there was nothing cooler than getting the privilege of walking around the empty Castle and helping it work. Between looking at the town and the beach, the beach was my preferred hang side. Over there, the Castle felt like a docked battleship waiting to set sail for the clear horizon. I imagined the pier would fold up like a collapsible drawbridge and the Castle would tear itself off from the pier columns like a giant tank. A floating, impenetrable fortress where I was the captain without a wheel. Onward! To nowhere!

Gazing down at the shoreline, I saw Melody stripping down to her bra and panties on the sand. It was far away enough so I couldn't really see details. But a panty-covered blur was better than nothing. She dove into the ocean and I had to be down there when she came out. I knew what happens to white when it gets wet. Immediately, I took off running through the Castle to get a closer look but I hit a flight of dark stairs, fell down them, and went lights out.

I don't know how long I was down but I woke up with someone stepping on me. It was a few cast members headed toward their stations in that wing of darkness.

"Whoa!" one of the voices said. "There's a body here!"

"Shut up," another said.

"No, check it out. Here."

I got stepped on again.

"Uggh, fuck," I said.

"Oh shit, it's a bum!" the second said.

"Dude, we don't want any trouble, just take off and it's all good."

"Yeah, man. Don't get weird."

"I work here, I'm… Dono," I finally said, getting up in the pitch black and trying to balance myself.

"Fuck, dude. You're hardcore. Are you partying tonight?"

"I don't know."

"Let's rage, dude. Meet at Brogi's, see you there," the other said.

"How will I know who you guys are?"

"Dude, we'll be the badass drunk guys with all the babes around us. Lates, bro."

"Lates, bro," another said.

"Lates, bros," I said, repeating the blind camaraderie. There's no way I could get into Brogi's but it was cool to pretend it was an option.

I rushed over to the makeup room to get into my custodial character.

"What happened to you?" Jack said, shaking a walkie-talkie.

"I fell and passed out."

"That'll happen." Jack laughed.

I couldn't tell if Jack believed me or not.

"Watch yourself. I don't need any more dead people in here."

Now, I really couldn't tell what Jack meant by the word "dead."

I wandered through the interior walls in mounting pain. My head was kinda alright but the sunburn seemed like it was getting more painful by the minute. And the itchy robe didn't help, no matter how cool it looked. I checked my traps from the day before. A whole new batch of dead rats had shown up. It was depressing. The charm of Castle Dunes was that one constantly escaped death. Whereas my job was to trap it. A guy dressed as a reaper is so much cooler than being a real one.

It inspired me to think of a way to shirk parts of the job I didn't like. Since the rats replaced themselves overnight in the traps, Jack wouldn't be able to tell that I'm not doing the job for a couple days. And he was a little wide to comfortably wander the interior walls to check. So I stopped the bagging and killing, and just wandered around doing whatever until some code got called.

I watched rooms from behind the red windows and studied the cast members. There were a few really bad ones who made me jealous I wasn't in their shoes. One guy wearing a straitjacket in the Madhouse room was practically catatonic. I swear he routinely pissed his pants because he never went on break, never said a word, never moved. He just stared intensely at every person who came through like each one was a better piece of meat. It was hard to tell how much of it was even an act. But it sucked, whatever it was. That guy would be perfect for cleaning up dead stuff.

After a few hours of doing my own thing in the Castle, I got bored and took my first break outside. I sat down at an empty table, spotted Renaldo, and called him over.

"Hey, bro, need anything?" he said.

"Nah, man. I just wanted to hang."

"I thought you'd ditch me once you became royalty, man, you're a good dude."

"Dude, I'm the custodian. I don't see the Castle rooms unless someone pukes or pisses in one. They give me a druid robe, some bleach, and paper towels. Not very royal."

He kept begging to hear stories about me banging chicks. I had to repeatedly tell him that it wasn't happening until he finally switched topics.

"I was thinking, we should start a band," he said.

"I don't know how to play anything."

"Dude, you can be the singer since you're tall."

"What do you play?"

"Nothing yet, but dude, I can just fuckin' sell my soul to Satan and turn into a shredder overnight! We will be so rad and famous, bro. You don't even know."

"Does that really work?"

"Oh, fuuuuck yeah, it does."

"How do you know?"

"Charlie, you know, from the Castle? Dude is satanic."

Made sense. Charlie actually played Satan in the Castle. He was a big guy and loved carrying his role with him wherever he went.

"Can he shred?"

"Nah, he asked for a bigger dick."

"He told you that? Did it work?"

"Dude, I'm not gay! How would I know? But yeah, he said it did and I didn't see it, but… I did see proof."

"Yeah?"

"At the time, he was bangin' the death rocker chick that plays Lizzie Borden and when he was telling me I was like, 'No way, bro,' but then she came out of the Castle and was walking all fucked up and he goes, 'See?' The only problem he says is that it's too big now and that's why she dumped him. And now he only bangs fat chicks 'cause their pussies are huge."

"Hm," I said while looking around. I needed to make sure no one witnessed me hanging out with a dude who'd just said that.

"Yeah, dude. My dick's big enough and I hate fat chicks so I'm like, fuck, dude, shred!"

"Hmmm." My eyes darted around again.

"Are you in?"

"I don't know what I'd sell my soul for. I don't want to be a singer."

"Dude, you gotta know something."

"I gotta think… the Castle."

"Bro, if you sell it to sing like King, you can basically make any other dream come true with your metal power. You can buy this place with your metal money. Best of both worlds. The band, man!"

"I don't know. How do you even do it?"

"I have this album and there's this one song where they just lay it right out, dude. It's so fucked up that you can only buy it as an import!"

"Whoa."

"Yeah, it's like the government knows this shit is real and they're just, like, no way."

I nodded. This made sense.

"We should test it out first," I said.

"Yeah, that's a good idea."

"What if we tried it with, like, a cat?"

"Wait, that would be like a sacrifice. Totally different," Renaldo said.

"No no, we won't kill him, we'll like just, like, broker his deal with the Devil."

"What should we sell the cat's soul for?"

"Maybe we should give it away for free. Like an appetizer," I suggested.

"That's a good idea. A cat's soul is probably worth, like, a penny in hell anyways."

"Dude, wait, what the fuck are we even talking about? This is ridiculous."

Renaldo ignored me.

"So now we need a bass player and a drummer. But they don't have to sell their souls."

"How come?" I said.

"Dude, 'cause it's just bass and drums. Who gives a shit about that? We're The Ones, dude!"

"Dude, I don't know if I want to sing. I want to work in the Castle. I want to be a monster."

"Shit, have you ever been to a metal show?"

"No."

"Fuck! That makes sense. Dude, there are monsters, castles, dragons, zombie robots, tits, booze—just like the Castle, but the music is waaaaay louder."

Dracula came outside and walked past our tables.

"What's up, Piss Bucket and Nacho Bitch," he said, sitting down at another table. Renaldo rolled his eyes and I kept silent.

Two permed-out high school girls ran up the employee ramp and ogled Dracula.

"It's you!" one of them squealed.

"The one and only," Dracula said, changing from mean asshole mode to aloof asshole mode.

"Can we get a picture?" the other girl said.

"Hey, Piss Bucket," Dracula said at me. "Take our picture."

They handed me the camera. The girls went to high school with me but I guess they couldn't tell who I was with the ghoul makeup on. Or they just didn't care. Dracula stood in between them and put his arms over their shoulders. Then without a second of hesitation, he put a hand on one of each girl's tits and said, "Smile." The girls didn't really know how to react. They were happy to be among celebrity but clearly didn't expect it to be so lecherous. One girl didn't seem to care as much as the other and said, "Thanks?" I wish I could have seen the developed photo.

One of the younger kids doing food runs saw his own opportunity. He came up to Dracula and asked for an autograph. He held out a Castle Dunes pennant with a marker.

Dracula didn't say anything and signed the kid's forehead instead of the pennant. The kid didn't know what to do and just stood there in confused disappointment.

"Why are you such a dick?" Renaldo said.

"Listen up, fuck face, I'm a dick and you're a pussy—so if you wanna keep it up, you're gonna get fucked."

"I always knew vampires were gay," Renaldo said.

Dracula got up and spit in Renaldo's face.

"I get more pussy than everyone in this whole town put together," Dracula said. "I'd unleash the fucking Drac attack on you right fucking now but I don't want beaner blood all over my makeup. This is your final warning."

Renaldo backed down and stared at the wood grain on the table. I hoped he was too high to give a shit, but it didn't seem like it.

The next few days brought more of the same for my custodial duties. To keep it interesting, I started to "work the environment" while attending to codes. Like, while kneeling by a dead rat to clean it up, a group of plebes came through and I pretended like I was eating it. It grossed them out and made me feel more involved. That helped pass the time, but I would have been so much more fulfilled if it was fake. Dracula kept calling Code Golds all day and night. I swear it was just to verbally abuse me. And I tried to plan breaks at the same time as Melody but always seemed to miss her.

While taking my makeup off one night, Jack came up and gave me a noogie on my head.

"You're off tomorrow, Dono."

"Oh, it's cool. I'll still come in."

"Nope."

"How come?"

"Because I'm not paying you seven days a week."

"I'll work seven days for five."

"Don't be a weirdo. Get out of here. Get some sun," Jack said, stuffing some cash in my hand. I never had that much money in my life. So my first thought was just to come right back to the Castle the next day and spend it.

I found Renaldo getting high under the pier and fanned my smile with the spread of bills.

"Nice, bro! Want to buy some weed?"

"Nah," I said. I was still high on the Castle's stage fog.

"Come on, don't fear the reefer!"

"Dude, I've got a day off and I owe you. Let's get some tickets and go in the Castle, on me."

"Man, it's the afternoon."

"So?"

"So, I'm still working," Renaldo said, motioning at the ocean. "And it's pointless. There's hardly anyone else there yet."

"That's good though. It's like you own it."

"No way, when it's packed I can cop a feel for forty-five minutes and get away with it. I try that shit out now and I'll get slapped or worse. Trust me, I know."

"Dude, come on."

"Dude, what's cooler? Fucking staring at some Castle bullshit or rubbing up on hot chicks?"

"Man, I don't know. It sounds kind of fucked up."

"Pfft! Ever felt some tits?"

"No."

"Well that could all change tonight."

I relented and waited until nightfall to go in the Castle with Renaldo. We hung out in front of it for what seemed like hours. I stared up at the facade, trying to dissect which exact rooms were where.

"Man, can we go in already? I'm actually starting to get sick of hearing the fucking 'Toccata,'" I said. Renaldo's eyes darted around the growing crowd of plebes.

"No. We gotta just wait outside until we see some hot chicks go in, then we jump in there behind them and…" Renaldo made a sex pumping motion.

"I don't want to wait forever, man," I said, getting impatient, thinking that I could have gone through a dozen times already.

Renaldo locked eyes on something over my shoulder.

"Timing… is… everything," he said.

I turned around and a group of three girls about our age approached the Castle. They seemed a little drunk and were all pretending to not want to be scared by the druids that flanked the entrance.

"Boom! Let's go," Renaldo said.

We lined up behind them and Renaldo was already trying the "I got pushed into you" trick on the girls. They weren't having it. In the darkest parts of the Castle, you could tell by their reactions how active Renaldo was with his hands. Hearing "Stop it!" mixed with "Ooo!" made me think he was only half a creep. A couple cast members recognized me and worked jokes in like "Clean up this lady's guts!" and "Welcome to the home of all the rat souls you've killed!"

Renaldo started getting more crude as the rooms went on though, and made me kind of embarrassed that I was with him. In the Headless Woman room, a mad doctor did a speech about how he had invented the perfect woman: a headless female that was a real woman propped up to hide her head. The doctor would try to pat her thigh and would get his hand smacked by the woman. Renaldo yelled out, "Finger her!" and that's when I took off into the next room, solo.

While in the Maze of Torment, one of the longest stretches of pure darkness in the Castle, I got my butt pinched and turned around, expecting Renaldo to be laughing his ass off. But a flashlight clicked on and illuminated Melody's face.

"Hey," she said, smiling.

I must have looked terrified because she laughed and clicked off her flashlight before quickly disappearing into the dark.

I was left standing in complete blackness with a thumping heart and half a boner. I kind of understood Renaldo's grab-ass run now. Fucking around in the Castle was exhilarating. The rest of the way through, I paid little attention to the scenery and focused on interpreting the butt pinch. The idea that I might have a real shot with her went from excitement to intimidation. I thought, "How am I going to fuck this up?"

When Renaldo and I met at the exit, we were both smiling.

"Dude, I think I felt up the whole fucking alphabet in there!" he said.

"Huh?"

"A cup, B cup, C cup, D cup!"

"Dude, even I got felt up."

"No way, did you punch him? Haha!"

"Dude! By a chick. Melody!"

"Oh nice, bro. Do you need to, like, throw out your underwear?"

"What? Dude, she just pinched my butt. But it was awesome."

"Your butt? Oh fucking please, man. You are way too hung up on that chick if you think that's exciting. Did you slap her titties around?"

"Jesus, man. Can you just let me have this one thing?"

"Yeah, yeah. Okay. But we should go through it again now, so you can slap her titties around."

"If I go through again, I'll look desperate."

"Dude, you are desperate. Fucking butt pinch, God."

"Dude, you know what? Fuck you."

"Bro, listen. I'm sorry but there's a whole fucking Castle full of witch bitches and horny plebes. Look over your shoulder, that's life passing you by."

I was torn. What he said seemed like it could be partially true but at the same time, I was happily hung up on this one chick and just wanted him to think it was rad. I could ditch Renaldo's friendship more easily than I could my feelings for Melody, but didn't want to do either.

"Can we skip the sermon and get something to eat?" I said, more pissed off than he'd seen me before.

"Bro, now you're talking," he said, trying to lighten the mood. "Let's see if there's any hair pies on the pier."

I couldn't help but laugh at his unwavering perversion. We grabbed some churros and sat down. Renaldo made a clear attempt at making me feel better about the Melody thing.

"She is pretty hot, dude," he said.

"Yeah, man."

"I wonder if her pussy hair is green too?" he asked.

"Dude! Jeez!" I said before pausing. "Hmmm actually, that's a good question."

I thought that being an off-the-clock plebe would reveal a new layer of the Castle's horror. Now that I had done it, I'd just become infatuated with butt pinches and pubic hair mysteries.

6

When Fourth of July rolled around, it was the most unhinged I had seen the Castle so far. Half of the cast members on duty were getting blown in the interior walls. Everyone was either drunk, stoned, or something'ed. In some areas, you couldn't tell what was stage fog and what was pot smoke. It wasn't just the cast members that were wasted. The plebes were even more out of control. Rowdy crowds poured through the Castle and tore the place up. Code Yellows and Greens everywhere.

I got a call to go to a pitch-black corner of a stairwell and clean up puke. When I got there, I used my flashlight to find the puke—but instead, I lit up Satan boning some hefty plebe chick. They didn't care that the puke was right next to them or that I had a flashlight, so I threw down the mop real quick.

"What's up, Dono," Satan said, pumping away.

"Hey, dude," I said and kept my eyes on the floor.

The girl tried to keep quiet. I turned my flashlight off and finished the job fast.

"Thanks, man, let's party later," Satan said in the dark.

It was officially the creepiest thing I'd ever seen in the Castle. But it quickly became the norm of the night. Anytime I'd go through the interior walls, there'd be monsters fucking each other or with some plebe or just some plebes. With the Fourth of July fireworks going off outside, it felt like a sex war inside. I was pinballing away from one and right into another. I realized how lame it was to stress over a butt pinch. I hadn't seen Melody yet, which made me glad at that point. I'd die if the Devil slayed her.

I had gotten a Code Gold a while ago but between the backed-up Greens and Yellows and having to take alternate routes in the walls, I was way late to respond.

"It's about fucking time, Piss Bucket," Dracula said, throwing his *Club International* porno mag at me.

"Dude, sorry. It's crazy tonight."

"Dude? Dude?! What the fuck do I look like? Do I look like a dude?" The half-empty bottle of scotch in the corner surrounded by a few beers let me know he was wasted.

"Dude, just, fuck, sorry… Colin."

He cocked his head.

"Uh, I mean Dracula. So give me the bucket?"

"You know what? Don't worry about that. Listen, I'm sorry about the way I've been acting. It's just, well, being the most important person in all of Castle Dunes comes with its own pressures."

"Uh, okay."

"Here, let me give you a beer," he said and handed me one from his stash.

Up to this point, I'd never had a beer handed to me and I thought a peace offering with Dracula was about the coolest way to do it. We toasted and I took a big slug, like when you tear into a soda. I took down half the can. But it wasn't anything like I expected. It was warm and totally not bubbly.

"Fuck, man, what beer is this? It tastes like piss," I said.

"It's called Drac Daniels."

"Oh… huh?"

"You dumb fuck, it is piss!" he said, laughing.

I gagged and threw the rest on the floor.

Dracula picked up the walkie-talkie.

"We've got a Code Yellow," he said in it and kicked up another round of laughs.

"What the fuck, man?" I said. "That's so fucked up. What

the fuck?" I didn't know what to do with myself because I wasn't a fighter. So I just stared at him in shock. He walked up to my chest and whispered, "Drac. Attack." And the red light signaling his performance turned on.

I slowly shuffled through an interior wall, so bummed. I had six ounces of piss in my stomach; should I puke it up? Is tasting it all over again, only grosser, better than digesting it? Is pissing Drac piss grosser than puking it? These questions seemed important. I just kept thinking about it and told myself that it's just there "for now."

My talents were being wasted. Being in the Castle was great but this Dracula shit was beyond a grind. I was ready to take a long, fuck-off break between the walls when my walkie blew up.

"Code Brown, Lizzy Borden."

It was Melody. I was glad for the excuse to see her but grossed out why. There were still hours left on the clock and the place was already exploding with every bodily fluid imaginable.

I got to Lizzie's Living Room where Melody was dressed up, sitting on the arm of a couch. It didn't seem dirtier than any other room in the Castle.

"You called a Code Brown?" I said.

"I'm just fucking with you! Let's do shots!"

I laughed and couldn't stop smiling. A cool, hot chick that's into funny, gross stuff.

"That'd be fucked-up though," she said.

"Yeah, this is like Anything Goes night."

"Hell yeah, it is."

Melody pulled a flask out from between the couch cushions. She flashed the whites of her eyes while taking a drink. I took the flask without hesitation and chugged it, not expecting what it would be like. The burn hit me hard and I started coughing as my face went red.

"Are you okay?" Melody asked, laughing.

The burn of the booze changed to a warm glow in my chest. It tasted like hell, but when I stopped coughing, I felt it kick in and looked up from my hands.

"I'm fucking awesome," I said. We were close enough to kiss but I was so frozen in rapture, I couldn't do anything. Melody smiled through her Lizzie makeup and didn't seem to feel weird at the silence that had formed. Was she waiting for more? My buzz had been confronted with a thick atmosphere of lust. Or love. While arguing with myself over whether to "go for it" versus "you'll get shut down," my walkie cut the tension.

"Code Somebody-Is-Passed-Out-in-the-Maze-of-Torment."

"Ha! I bet it's one of us," Melody said.

Us.

"Yeah, I should probably go check that."

As I was leaving, I told her, "Take it out." What the fuck was that? What did I just say? Take it out? Take what out? I had tripped on my tongue. I meant to say take it easy or over and out, but they smashed together in a horrific accident. My eyes went wide at the wreckage.

"Huh?" she asked.

I didn't actually want to leave but I needed to get out of there before I said anything else dumb or desperate.

"I gotta take this out," I said nodding to my scooper. She looked at me like she was thinking, "How did this get weird?" I began to quickly walk out of the room. The shot may have loosened me up, but it didn't exactly make me cool.

"Hey," she said, stopping me. "So what are you doing tonight?"

"Nothing." No one asks you what you're doing and then doesn't invite you to something. I had seen it unfold a million times at school. Always without me.

"Nothing? It's Fourth of July. Let's party, dude!"

"Awesome, yeah," I said as the blood began draining out of my head.

"Meet ya out by the tables after work."

"Tables," was all I could say. It was all too easy. It was more believable that I was being set up as a joke. Did chicks just lay it out like that? Did it mean she wanted to hang like friends or hang like boyfriend and girlfriend? Any of it was better than none of it though. I had to figure out how I was going to act when this all went down. I had to consider all sorts of personalities. Which one would she like the best? Should I go with a cool type of thing? Or should I go with a more badass personality maybe? I just needed to be the guy who didn't have a heart attack.

Later on, I got "Code Gooold" on the walkie. I wouldn't respond. Why would I? Fuck Dracula. I decided to take my break instead. But Jack found me at the tables and said, "Is your walkie broken or can you not handle the job?"

The only way I could deal with it was by reminding myself that there was only an hour of work left. When I showed up behind the mantel, Dracula was getting blown by some chick. His cape covered her up and he was totally more plowed than before.

"Oh, sorry," I said and began to leave.

"No, you stay here," he said with a smirk. He didn't seem pissed at all. The girl tried to turn around but Dracula said, "Don't stop." She got up anyway and ran off. Dracula didn't seem to care.

"Another day at the Castle, huh?" he said, nodding to the bucket. I looked in it and there were four used rubbers floating inside.

This guy had everything, so what the fuck was his problem? It was the first day that made me ready to get the fuck out of the Castle at the end of the night. At least for a few hours.

When I got to the tables, I instantly realized that whatever I was doing with Melody wasn't a real date or anything. Too good to be true, of course. There was a group of drunk cast members and Renaldo, all ready to keep partying.

"Donovan!" Melody shouted. I already knew a bunch of the other cast members. They all seemed pumped that I was going to join them, which made it the biggest group of people I had ever hung out with.

"Hey, so, we're going to Brogi's. Are you ready? I hope you're wearing your pocket pants," Melody said.

"What? Oh, ha. Shit, yeah, I can't get in."

Renaldo cut to the front of the group.

"No, but JJ can!" he said.

"Who's JJ?"

"You!" he said, pulling out a fake ID. It said "JJ Doobie" on it and had my twenty-first birthday as tonight. I had gone from sixteen to eighteen to twenty-one in the blink of an eye.

"No way, dude! You rule," I told Renaldo.

"Fuck yeah, I do. Let's get wasted."

"Are you sure it'll work?"

"Dude, you could flash a coupon at Brogi's and get in."

We all walked over to the bar and Melody came up alongside me.

"Hey, so happy birthday, JJ," she said and kissed me on the cheek. It left an outline of lip gloss that I wasn't about to wipe off. Maybe this was a date? Melody was so untethered. The only thing concrete about her was all the free-floating ambiguity. I wanted to lasso it or become it, whichever came first. I wasn't confident I could do either.

"Doobie. JJ Doobie," Renaldo said like James Bond. I looked

over at him the way you do at someone you're riding a roller coaster with, just about to take the big drop.

We got to the front door and the bouncer guy out front carded everyone. I was second to last with Renaldo behind me and handed my new ID over.

"JJ Doobie? That's your real name?" the bouncer said.

"Yeah."

"You look more like a Suds LeBrewski," he said, laughing.

I stood there and waited for the blow of disappointment.

"I was born on—" I said.

"Whatever, dude. This is the best fake ID I've seen in a while. Come on in."

And just like that, I stepped from the all-ages concrete sidewalk and into my first bar that didn't double as a restaurant. The place was a dive, bathed in wood panels and red lights. The bar saved all their Halloween beer promotion signs from years past and kept them up permanently. The cast members washed off their roles with an avalanche of beers and shots but it was more like shape-shifting. No matter how wasted they got, you could see traces of their characters still lingering in their off-the-clock personalities. The gleam of a demon's eye or the over-confidence of an executioner. But everyone was in a good mood and it was infectious. I'd already had the one shot at the Castle and wanted to be part of the team. Not under the bleachers. Not on the sidelines. But actually in it.

Melody bought me a beer and Renaldo made everyone sing happy birthday to me, including "Jaaaaay Jaaaaaay" as my name at the end of it.

Two chicks bet some dude cast members that they couldn't do ten shots in a row. If they did, the prize was that they'd show their tits.

"JJ, you want to get in on this?" the Satan guy said.

Melody waited for my response.

"Nah, I already did like twenty shots and Melody showed her third nipple."

"Okay, buddy. Stand back."

Our group chanted the shot numbers out and they actually made it to ten. The chicks went to lift their shirts up at the same time Satan barfed and fell over.

I leaned over to Melody while keeping my eyes on the chicks. "This is the greatest night ever."

"Oh you like that, huh?" she said.

"Oh, I mean, no. No. I think this stuff is degrading."

"I bet."

Renaldo and I dragged Satan out to the parking lot and propped him up on the curb. He seemed comfortable passed out on the concrete, so we left him there. As we were about to walk in, Renaldo spotted Dracula's car.

"Dude, check it out, that's Colin's," he said. The car was rocking back and forth.

"Is he banging in there?"

"Looks like."

"Let's fuck with him," I said.

"Hell, yeah. I like your style, JJ," Renaldo said, pulling a long strand of firecrackers out of his pocket.

"Give me that shit." Renaldo handed me a lighter too. We crept up alongside Colin's car and crouched down below the backseat windows. They were cracked just enough so they wouldn't fog up and we could hear him inside talking to some chick.

"Yeah, baby, I'm the one from the commercial," he said as the car bounced up and down.

"Ohhh," the girl said.

"And I vant to suck… your tits," Colin said in his shitty Dracula accent.

Renaldo and I had to cover our mouths to keep from cracking up but didn't do that great of a job.

"What the fuck was that?" he said as the rocking stopped.

"I didn't hear anything," the girl moaned and started the motion up again.

I lit the huge strand of Black Cat firecrackers and threw them through the gap in the window. We ran like hell as we heard, "What the fuck! What the fuck!" and frantic scrambling. Renaldo and I got to the curb in front of Brogi's, next to where Satan was passed out, and turned around. The fireworks went off loud as hell and lit up the backseat. The back door swung open. Colin tried to jump out but his pants were around his ankles and he fell on his face. The butt-naked chick he was with scrambled over him and disappeared off into the night. Renaldo and I were dying laughing as Colin cocked his head up.

"You could have fucking killed me!" he yelled. It seemed like he was trying not to cry at the same time.

"Dude, it wasn't me," I said.

"Wasn't me," Renaldo said.

The bouncer stepped between us and said to Colin, "Wasn't me. Now get out of here before I call the cops on you for public indecency."

It turned out that the bouncer and Renaldo had been tight for years. When I asked Renaldo why the dude was so cool, he just cryptically answered that he'd saved the bouncer's life once. I could relate to that.

Colin jumped in the driver's seat and peeled out of the parking lot as he screamed, "You're fucking dead!"

We went back into the bar and kept celebrating my fake birthday and our small victory. The cast members were a blast to hang with and, as simple as it may sound, drinking kicked ass. I was a lot more talkative with Melody and things seemed to be going well. Not even Renaldo's crude interruptions could derail it.

"Hey… Melody," he said, leaning in close to her. "Donovan—I mean, JJ—has a huge dick. You should totally suck it."

All the beers made me laugh instead of cringe.

"How would you know?" she said.

"Heard some chicks talking."

"Oh, yeah?" she said, looking at me. I couldn't tell if she was suspicious or turned on.

"No way, nobody has ever seen my dick." I thought my defense was good until I realized it was an admission of virginity.

"Dude!" Renaldo said.

"Shit! That's not what I meant, I mean, like, I'm not… doing…"

"Ha! You guys are retarded," she said. "Wanna get out of here?" she asked me. "It's almost closing and I hate it when the lights come on."

"Uh, yeah," I said and took her hand and started for the door.

"Suck that shit!" Renaldo yelled while headbanging us out.

We both stumbled out to the sidewalk but I was definitely drunker than she was. She took her flannel off and revealed a skin-tight shirt with a giant pot leaf on it.

"You wanna go smoke in the dunes?" she asked. I stared at her shirt and was finally convinced that pot was for me.

"Totally."

We walked past the Castle and hit the sand dunes just on the other side. It was kind of funny that the town was named after them. I don't think our founding fathers knew they'd just be used for drugs and sex. Tonight, the dunes were already teeming with people making out and doing illegal shit. We waded through a few clusters of people to find our own valley.

Melody flopped down on the sand and pulled out a joint. I still had Renaldo's lighter so I thought it'd be cool if I tried to light it for her. I was so drunk I couldn't get it to work in the easy breeze and flicked it over and over.

"Here," she said, taking it from me and lighting it in one stroke. She took a long draw off the joint and passed it to me.

"It's almost a full moon," she said.

I looked up at the night sky and took a big toke off the joint.

"Yeah."

That's the last thing I remembered before blacking out.

7

I woke up the next morning in the daze of another planet. Hot and sandy, this environment was incapable of sustaining life. My own existence seemed like an illusion. My pants were around my ankles and I was alone. Was this death? I had no idea if something very good or very bad had happened. The alone part made it seem bad though. At least my boxers were still on.

Wait, now I remembered Melody. Where was she?

I pulled my pants up and brushed the sand off. I walked up the dune nearest to the ocean to get a better view of my crash site.

When I got to the top I saw Melody, swimming in the ocean in her bra and panties.

"Come in!" she yelled with her arms up as a small wave hit her back.

I tore my pants back off, ran past the blackened shells of spent fireworks, and plunged into the ocean.

"Are you as hungover as I am?" she said.

"I think I'm still drunk."

Melody laughed and swam up to me. I went to kiss her, but she hesitated.

"I didn't brush my teeth," she said.

"I've never brushed my teeth ever," I joked.

Melody laughed and put her arms around me. We kissed for the first time. Or again, I guess. Due to the blackout, I had no clue what my current experience level was.

She grabbed a piece of skin that was peeling from my old sunburn and pulled it off.

"You're shedding," she said. I thought it was gross but she seemed to like it.

"What happened last night?" I asked.

"Like what?"

"Like what did we do?"

"We went to Brogi's."

"I remember that."

"Then we went to the dunes."

"I don't remember that."

"We smoked a joint and played Who Can Make the Scariest Face? You won. Then we made out for a while. You're a good kisser, you know. And then you passed out while trying to take your pants off."

"Fuck. Really?"

"Yeah."

"That's it?"

It still sounded like a pretty awesome night even if my brain wasn't around to remember it. I tried constructing the memory in my head for something to savor.

"Oh, and you said you love me," Melody said.

"Whoa." I couldn't tell if I said "whoa" out loud or in my head. I was embarrassed. But she didn't say it like it was a bad thing. She also didn't say she felt the same. But she didn't run away, so it could've been worse.

"Are you working today?" she asked.

"Yeah, you?"

"I'm gonna ditch. Still celebrating independence," she said while leaning back and floating in the water.

"Is Jack gonna be pissed?"

"Nah. What's one less witch in the Castle?"

I showed up for roll call and the first thing Jack said was "Look at my face because I'm fucking pissed!" Only fifteen people showed up. It took at least thirty and at best fifty people to properly operate Castle Dunes. Almost everyone from yesterday went to sleep at dawn but had failed to rise. Or they were off eating breakfast burritos somewhere with their head in their hands, feeling more inhuman than the roles they couldn't face. Who could blame them? Being locked inside a sweltering castle all day, listening to horror soundtracks and provoking screams, would be Code Green central.

"Well, this day is going to be shit," Jack continued, "and unfortunately for you guys that showed up, you're gonna get the short end. We can't do breaks today, I can't lose anyone."

Everyone got bummed. The heat was already brutal in the morning and it was only going to get worse. Jack assigned the roles, and everyone shuffled into the Castle.

I was still trying to stop my brain from sloshing around when Jack locked eyes with me.

"Hey, Dono, since I'm running a circus of unreliable drug addicts and alcoholics, I need you to fill in as a cast member."

I stood in silent shock.

"Does that stupid look on your face mean okay?"

"Yes."

"Follow me."

Jack led me into the costume room and pulled a Wolfman mask out of a box. It stunk like hell. He handed me wolf hands too, and I put the hairy claws on first. Just then, Dracula came into the room.

"What the fuck?!" Dracula said, raising his arms. "Some piss-bucket, nacho bitch comin' in on my stage? My stage? This is unacceptable, Jack."

"Easy, Colin," Jack said. "We're too short staffed for this today."

Dracula kept at it.

"This fucking piece-of-shit kid almost killed me last night."

Jack was unresponsive. Dracula pressed a finger into my chest.

"Drac. Attack. Motherfucker."

"We don't have time for that shit," Jack said. Dracula ignored him.

"Just watch it," he told me and clipped my shoulder while storming off.

"So what'd you do to him last night?" Jack said.

"Threw firecrackers in his car while he was making it."

"Ha!" Jack slapped my back.

I pulled the Wolfman mask over my head.

"Okay, you're gonna be doing a thug role," he said. "Means you don't have to speak. Just jump scares. You won't have to worry about riffing dialogue. Can you act like a werewolf?"

I looked into the mirror at my furry face, assumed the lurching attack pose of a werewolf, and let out a howl.

"Great, now it gets hot with that shit on. So make sure you drink lots of water and pop one of these every now and then."

Jacked handed me some white pills.

"Uh, what are these?"

"Ha, you wish. They're salt pills. It's so you don't get heatstroke. Take them."

I pocketed the pills and adjusted my mask.

"This thing smells like shit."

"Yeah, I think the last guy died in it, sorry, pal!"

I couldn't tell if he was joking or not. I was all suited up and admired myself in the mirror. Jack put his arm around me and looked in the mirror too.

"Like father, like son!" Jack said with a belly laugh. "I still think I'm hairier though."

Jack took me to the Haunted Forest room. It was densely packed with fake trees and had a mossy rock to hide behind.

"Alright, real simple. Hide behind the rock and when you hear someone come in, pop out, act like you're going to kill 'em and chase 'em into the next room."

I gave a thumbs up. Jack flipped a switch behind a curtain and left. "Forest at Night" sounds thickened the atmosphere.

It was a quick room. Some were meant to be longer. This one was just a classic shock scare, or a "boo room." Non-speaking roles were featured less often in the Castle but were the most important in keeping the place scary. The set-piece rooms were spooky looking but mostly funny. They weren't able to actually make you jump in fright like a properly timed shock from the dark.

I positioned myself behind the rock and waited for people to come through. Before any did, I was already drenched in sweat from being trapped under wolf skin. The mouth allowed little room for the passage of air, so I had to make my breathing deliberate. It was a slow start to the day since the rest of the town seemed to have ditched everything too. The longer I waited, the more nervous and scared I felt about a customer coming through.

Finally, I heard screams come from the room before me and psyched myself up. Three teenagers ran into my room and stopped in the middle of it.

"This room sucks," one said.

"Yeah, why's there a forest in a castle anyways?" the second said.

"There ain't shit in here, keep—"

I burst out from behind the rock, swinging my arms wildly, and let out a scream that was way too high pitched to be scary.

"Hahahaha, Wolfman sucks!"

Embarrassed, I waited for the next group while continuously coughing to make sure my throat was clear.

Next, I got a good scare in. It freaked the shit out of the plebes and they ran through the room, clutching each other's shoulders in front of them. With a simple and strong "Arrrrggghh" I had turned a room that sucks into one to run from. And transformed myself into a minimum-wage walking terror.

I repositioned myself and waited. It was a good thing I had a mask on to hide my less-than-terrifying, beaming smile.

The job didn't take much, just good timing. I repeated the scare over and over. It worked better on some than others. Customers' comments ranged from "Fuck!" to "Fuck you!" Either one was a reaction, which was all I was looking for.

The day's heat dragged on, slow and thick, but I had a blast in the Wolfman loop. It took a while just for my shoulders to drop and accept that this was all actually happening. Everything was so good, how could it actually be real?

After lunchtime, a wave of people holding black and white fliers passed through. I knew the Castle didn't distribute anything and wondered where they were coming from.

No one passed through for a half hour, then my Haunted Forest started to fill up with the smell of weed. I left my post behind the rock and poked my werewolf head into the Phantom of the Opera room before me. Raw and aggressive heavy metal blasted out of the room's speakers. I didn't remember any metal in the Castle before. A disfigured, caped man pretended to play an organ while puffing a joint. Fake blood came from his ears and ran down his neck. This setup was supposed to explain where the "Toccata" outside was coming from, had it been playing in the room.

"Hey, dude," I said. The Phantom couldn't hear me. I placed my paw on him.

"Jesus fucking Christ!" The Phantom turned around, choking on his smoke.

"Hey, sorry," I said.

"Who the fuck are you?"

"I'm a werewolf," I said.

"No, who. The. Fuck. Are. You."

"Oh, I'm Dono."

"You're new?"

"Yeah, kinda."

"I'm Rex."

"What's the music?" I said, nodding up to the speakers.

"My band," he said and motioned to a stack of fliers on the organ. "Here, check us out," he said, handing me one. I looked down and it was a collage of skeletons having sex in every imaginable position. It read: TION—AT THE DITCH! and had some info details.

"Tee-I-On?" I pronounced.

"No, dude, it's Tion," he said, pronouncing it like "shun."

"Tion. What's that?" I said.

"It's the most metal name in the world."

"How come?"

"Dude, it's the most commonly rhymed syllable in all of metal."

"I don't get it."

"Like," Rex said, grasping for an invisible mic and making a metal face, "I'll kill you by decapita-*tion*! You're death is hallucina-*tion*! No need for the prosecu-*tion*! Our metal is a revela-*tion*!"

"Oh, okay, cool."

"Yeah. And that's what our record is gonna be called too," he said, nodding with confidence.

"Tion. Like self titled?"

"No, shun. Like shunned."

"Like the name, but Tioned?"

"Fuck man, you'll get it when you see the cover."

"Sweet. Do—"

He cut me off. "Wait, shhh. Check out this tom roll."

I listened as the drummer made a lengthy fill that sounded like someone falling down a flight of stairs.

"Yeah, bro," he said, air drumming and nodding along.

A group of teenage plebes came through, and Rex sprang into action with fliers.

"Welcome to my crypt of musical death. Like music? Hear now my symphony of the catacombs. Check out my band," he said, handing out the fliers.

The kids were confused why the Phantom was in a local metal band and hanging out with a casual werewolf.

"Why's the Wolfman here?"

"Because metal soothes the savage beast," Rex said. "See how complacent it's made him? Hey, if you like true metal, check out my band. We're playing The Ditch," he said.

"Your band sucks," one of them said and dropped the flier on the floor.

I jumped on the opportunity and flared into a violent Wolfman rage, chasing them out of the room and past mine.

I retreated behind my mossy rock with a flier in my hand and looked at it more closely. Tion at The Ditch. Alright, I'm in. Maybe I could get Melody to go.

Rex poked his head into the Haunted Forest.

"Thanks, bro," he said and flashed the devil horns at me. "But seriously, check my band out."

I went back to work with the werewolf act and finished the day with strobed-out eyes and the taste of stage fog in the back of my throat. I never wanted to go back to picking up turds again. I was a plebe a couple of weeks ago and now a famous monster. A professional exhibit. Holding this newly appointed power ruled. But I was also in disbelief of it. Finally running with the pack, I just hoped they didn't eat me alive at the first sign of weakness.

8

I told Jack it was the best day of my life and he threw a T-shirt at my face. I unfolded it. It read "Castle Dunes Cast Member" in Old English letters and had a sketch of the Castle on the front.

"Welcome aboard, Wolfman. I heard good things about you today. You're our new substitute for any roles that go abandoned for whatever reason."

I went to hug Jack and as I did, he poured a beer on my head.

"That's how Castle Dunes hugs," he said, laughing more than usual. I loved it. I had been baptized. I wondered if "any roles that go abandoned" also meant Dracula's post.

I didn't take that shirt off for the rest of the summer. It was my new family crest. If I was walking around the pier or town and someone said "Nice shirt!" I could be like, "Yeah, I totally work there. No big deal," and just blow their mind. No one ever said that, but I was ready if they did.

I did the Wolfman job for a couple more days and even though I repeated the same action over and over, I loved it. It was a cathartic loop, howling at a painted moon. But it made me restless after hours. I wanted to keep going, tearing shit up and screaming at people more than ever.

"You wanna go fuck shit up?" Renaldo asked with a secretive nod and a baseball bat in hand. I was still riding the Wolfman buzz after work and didn't want to go home anytime soon.

"What do you mean?" I said.

"C'mon, let's go."

Renaldo took me down the Dunes coast to a new tract of homes on Sea Grave Road that were about seventy percent finished. They had windows, roofs, and walls without paint, but no carpet, doors, or any finishing details. The recently paved road was sporadically lined with Porta Potties for construction workers. Renaldo picked up a stray two-by-four and handed it to me.

"Here's yours. Let's go."

I took the long piece of wood and followed him inside one of the houses. It didn't smell like any house I'd been in before. There was no stench of Lean Cuisine, suffocating dryer sheets, perfumed laundry detergent, or stale cigarette smoke. It smelled like a hardware store and a lumber yard put together.

"Watch out for nails and shit, dude," Renaldo said, bolting up the stairs. "Okay, check it out. See this wall?"

It was a freshly finished drywall in the master bedroom.

"Yeah," I said, still unsure where this was going. Kind of.

"These walls are total shit. Take a swing, dude."

"You first," I said.

"Batter up!" Renaldo yelled and swung for the bleachers right into the wall. The bat pierced the drywall with a thud and stuck there.

"Ha! See, man? Now you."

Fuck it, why not? I swung and ripped a hole into the wall next to Renaldo's. I immediately felt the satisfaction of destruction.

"Good one, dude," Renaldo said and took another swing of his own. I didn't need to be invited twice. We were both attacking the walls of the master bedroom like they were closing in on us. We moved on to smashing up the whole place. We broke every single window, dry toilet, and mirrored closet in sight. We even poked holes in the ceiling, laughing our asses off as we got covered in powdery drywall.

"You look like a ghost," I said, out of breath.

He held up a shard of mirror to his face. "I look like a fucking white dude," he laughed. "Hey, there's twenty-nine more houses. Wanna fuck up another?"

"Hell, yeah, man. This is way radder than I thought it was gonna be."

"Right?"

We went into another house a few doors down. They were all exactly the same inside and out. My approach to house number two was more experienced and scientific. I ran around the first floor bashing out windows like I was being timed for it. I could hear Renaldo doing the same upstairs. Each time I broke something, I felt better. I don't know what about, but it was good. And the more I did it, the more calm I felt. Proud even. Renaldo came downstairs.

"Nice work down here, I really like what you've done to the place," he said.

For some reason, that was funnier than it should have been and I couldn't stop laughing.

We went outside, and I viewed the Porta Potties much differently than before. I ran up to one and pushed it over. The door swung open and a flood of blue fluid poured out on the ground.

"Fucking sweet!" Renaldo ran to do the same to another.

We eventually tipped every single one over and sat down on the curb. Renaldo lit up a joint and we passed it back and forth.

"Dude, we should do this, like, all the time," I said.

"Yeah, I know. But we can't. It has to be random. Or else they hire a security guard and then you're screwed if you get caught."

"Have you, like, ever slept here before?"

"Nah, I don't want to wake up with a gun in my face."

"Yeah, no. Good point. I should take Melody here."

"Chicks don't like smashing things."

"I mean… to, like, smash her." After raging in the Castle all day and tearing up the neighborhood all night, I was ready to get more aggressive with everything.

"Ha! Nice. But I don't think she'd dig it, bro. Plus, I don't want everyone finding out and coming in my homes, fucking them up."

I needed to book more time with Melody. The kiss was cool but I was going for a promotion. I figured it went well in the water last time, why not try again? So we went swimming before work. I had always avoided it in the past, but now with Melody, the beach started to make a lot more sense. We floated around close to the pier. Raised on the columns, the Castle was even taller when looking up at it from the water. You could hear the occasional scream as someone ran out of the Castle exit. The "Toccata." People laughing on the pier. Bells ringing out of carnival booths.

"What do you want to be when you grow up?" Melody said.

"Shit, I'm doing it already."

"You don't want to do that."

"What do you mean?"

"Look at Colin, he's been here for years. He's fucked now."

"Seems like he's got it made."

"Are you kidding? This is just a summer job. You know what he does the rest of the year?"

"I dunno." Ever since I first laid eyes on the Castle, I hadn't thought about any other future.

"He's a busboy at Ye Olde Times," she said.

Ye Olde Times was a Renaissance-themed dinner and tournament experience two towns over. I guess it was cool but not really.

"So what do you really want to do?" she asked.

"Make horror movies then." It seemed like the same thing to me.

"Horror movies hate me," she said.

"What do you mean?"

"If drinking, smoking pot, and having sex means you deserve to die, then I'm screwed."

We both laughed and started making out in the water. I kinda went from being the guy who survives in the movie to the one who dies too. Not kinda. I wanted to be that guy. It had become my goal.

"Up there," she said, nodding to the Castle, "I can be the bad guy. I can scare the shit out of some big idiot and make him run. Well, you know."

I remembered a night ago when I scared the shit out of a school bully by calling his name out. Harmless yet thoroughly satisfying vengeance.

"I wish I could invite everyone I ever knew that was a dick to me to the Castle, terrorize the living hell out of them, and make them pay for the pleasure," I said. "I wouldn't even need to scream in their face. I could do live Mirror of Death oracles that would make them cry."

"Sounds kinda angry there," she said.

"Nah…" I didn't think it was my anger. It was the Castle's. I would just be filling a role that wielded it. A perfect fit in my mind, but Melody's eyes looked sympathetic.

"Anyways," I said. "What's the gnarliest thing that's ever happened to you in the Castle?"

"I was playing a dead schoolgirl role and speaking in a little girl's voice, when this older guy came in by himself and I went, 'Daddy? It's me. Why did you make me cry?'"

"Creepy."

"Yeah, totally. And he grabbed his chest and fell to the floor. Had a heart attack right there. Oops."

"Jesus Christ, did he die?"

"No, but how messed up is that? I don't do that anymore. What's the gnarliest thing that ever happened to you in the Castle?"

Should I tell her? Should I say it? Fuck it.

"You," I said.

Melody smiled and went underwater. I couldn't see where she was. After a dozen long seconds, I thought I might have sunk her somehow. Like, tell a girl how you feel and then they turn to stone. But she popped back up, right in front of me.

"Why are you so nice to me?" she said. She had her bathing suit bottoms in her hand and wrapped her legs around my waist.

"Whoa," I said as she grabbed my dick with the most devious smile I had ever seen. Alright, the only devious smile I had ever seen. I immediately looked up to the pier and saw various people looking over the edge, taking in the view of the beach. And possibly us. I couldn't tell, but some had to be.

She moved herself into position.

"We can't do it in front of everyone!" I said.

"No one knows what we're doing. We're hugging."

"You've got your bottoms in your hand."

"Who gives a fuck what people think?" It was Melody's theme song and I was starting to learn the words. She pressed herself down on me and I didn't give a fuck what people thought.

Quickly after it started, it ended. We put our bottoms on underwater, swam to shore, and flopped down on the sand.

"That was awesome," I said.

Melody kissed me again. We laid back and stared at the sun through our closed eyelids. My mind was still spinning over what just went down. I opened an eye and leaned on my elbow.

"Can I ask you a question?" I said.

"Uh oh."

"How many guys have you slept with?"

Melody looked disappointed.

"Or, you know, swam with?" I clarified.

"Why does it matter?"

"Well, 'cause if it's a lot, then I probably suck compared to some of those dudes. And I'd rather you didn't know I sucked."

"You can't go off that," she said, nodding to the ocean. "Everyone knows fucking in the water sucks, but it's better than not fucking in the water."

I pretended to know.

"So you don't think I suck?"

"If that were true, I wouldn't be here."

"What do you mean?"

"I mean, I like you. Why are you trying to find a problem with that?"

It was assuring, but also a bummer to know that I could be poisoning the well for no reason.

"Thanks. I'll hit the suck brakes. Forget I said anything."

"What's that?"

"Forget I said anything."

"What's that?"

"Ha, I get it."

I wasn't sure I was getting anything. Having sex wasn't like turning a page or starting a new chapter. It was like setting the whole book on fire. I was becoming close with two people who were strangers to me just a month ago: Melody and myself. And I didn't really know where either was going.

After that, I showed up early to roll call. Jack was there reading his clipboard and looked up at me.

"Fucking with the fishes, huh?" Jack said.

"What do you mean?" My cheeks went red.

"Think no one noticed? Ha!"

"Shit, how'd you know?"

"I saw you guys from the pier. Hey, I don't care. You've got some balls to slay a chick in the water in front of everyone. Ocean sex sucks though, am I right? And how can it be so dry feeling when it's in the goddamn water?"

"Yeah, it sucked." No it didn't. But him, and probably others, witnessing my devirginization did suck.

"Let me ask you something, Dono," Jack said in a rare tone reserved for casual, non-Castle–related issues.

"Yeah."

"I know you're having fun, but you wearin' a rubber out there?"

"No, I did," I said. I didn't want to disappoint him.

"Bullshit," he said. "You know how I know?"

"Not really."

"It's impossible to fuck in the ocean with a rubber. I should know."

"Sorry."

"Listen, I'm not gonna lie to you. Wearing a rubber doesn't feel as good as barebackin' it. But you know what feels better than unprotected sex?"

I was listening to Jack but he expected an answer. There was no answer.

"Do ya?" he said.

"No."

"I'll tell you. Freedom. Freedom feels better than anything. When you use a condom, you maintain your freedom. Don't use a condom? Knock a chick up before you should? Trouble, no matter what happens. You ready for that? No freedom? Now your life sucks and no amount of hot sex can make it better. Only worse! Wearing a condom is like raising a flag. Yours. Stock up on flags, Dono." Jack slapped my back a little less harder than usual and walked away.

I really locked that into my head. Janice might have given birth to me and provided my partial survival ever since then, but somehow I could easily trust Jack more. I didn't even know I had this freedom in the first place. But now in the moment, my mind began to race. Did I already sacrifice my freedom? Before I even knew what I was doing? It really didn't even occur to me in the ocean. I didn't plan it and she didn't care, so neither did I. I promised myself I would heed Jack's advice, but I needed to find out if I had already blown it.

I was supposed to report to Wolfman duty in the Haunted Forest but I had to find Melody. I caught up with her in the Witch's Cauldron room.

"Hey, what are you doing here?" she asked.

"Hey. I've gotta talk to you."

"Oh, jeez," she said.

"No, not like that," I said.

"Like what?"

"Like should I have had something on when we were in the ocean?"

"Sunblock?" she asked.

"No! Like a… condom."

"Oh, it's cool. Don't worry about that," she said.

"So you're not pregnant?"

"Jesus, Donovan, how old are you?"

That's right, I was eighteen to her. What would an eighteen year old say?

"Shit, just tryin' to be nice. I'm really tired and work's been grinding my ass." I had reverted to Renaldo's old-means-complaining advice.

"Yeah. Well, thanks. I guess we should get working," she said.

"Yeah, see you after."

She didn't say anything. Maybe she didn't want to see me after, so I extended the time range.

"I mean later," I said. I was out of my league. Total amateur vibe. I really needed to provide some evidence that I didn't give a fuck before leaving. I turned around, and while walking toward the next room, cut a huge cheek ripper of a fart. *Brrrraaaappppp!* Melody burst into more laughter than I'd ever heard. I kept walking as she kept laughing. Success.

After work, Renaldo asked me if I'd get him a Lotto ticket at the liquor store since he was banned from it.

"Can't win if you don't play," he said when I asked him why he wanted one. "I'd buy so much shit."

"What about buying it with metal power?"

"Huh?"

"You were talking about selling your soul to shred and the band and shit."

"What? Fuck, man. I must have been high as hell. I'm no organ donor to the Devil, man. Fuck that shit. Dude, Lotto."

"What would you do if you won?" I asked.

"Oh, bro. Everything. I'd get a giant mansion where porn star chicks would live with me. Anything they want for anything I want. I'd buy the Arena Dome up north and make it a metal-only venue, where all the tickets are free. And I'd sell beer for high fives. I'd scour the Amazon with a team of scientists looking for the world's most killer weed. Then I'd drop the seeds from a plane flying all over America so forests of it grow everywhere. I'd have a charity where fucked-up metal kids, like retards or dying dudes, could have their number one metal wish happen. I'd buy the world's biggest record store as my own record collection. I'd buy a mountain and carve my face into it. Fuck, man. Everything. How 'bout you?"

"Castle Dunes."

"Dude, the Castle? I mean, it's cool. But dude, porn stars don't want to live in that."

"I'd live there with Melody," I said. She was already pretty much living there anyways.

"Dude, the Castle and Melody? Pick something that lasts, man. Dream big."

I thought I was dreaming big.

When the Tion show came, I was off. Renaldo had a big pre-game plan for us to get wasted. I wanted to make it like a date with Melody and told him I'd have to meet him there and then hang. He got all pissed.

"Dude, what's the difference if we just cruise together? I sell that chick weed all the time man, we're cool."

"I want it to be like something more official than what we've been doing."

"Dude, metal shows aren't about going with chicks. They're about going with bros to rage with and listening to pro-bros sing about chicks."

"Dude, what?"

"But then if you meet a chick at the show, that's cool."

Renaldo was being serious but I laughed.

"Man, whatever," I said. "We're going to hang. I just need a little pre-hang."

"Fine, dude, then I'll see you in the pit! I'll be the motherfucker tearing it up!"

It turned out that it didn't matter. I ended up going solo because I couldn't get hold of Melody. I didn't know if I was being paranoid, but she seemed pretty elusive for a person I recently had sex with in public.

The Ditch wasn't a club. It was a ditch. A hollowed out piece of land on the edge of town that was an abandoned site originally planned for a supermarket. The cops had no reason to go that far on patrol, so it was perfect for people to do whatever in. The band set up against one of the dirt walls and made a stage of plywood scattered on the dirt floor. It looked like a suburban archeological dig or a mass grave. Or just a local metal show, I guess. There were already about a hundred people there crowded around three kegs.

I spotted Melody's hair quickly and walked up behind her. She was being really talkative with one of the dudes in the band. I wasn't sure how to interrupt. I wasn't drunk enough to act as cool as I needed to, so I retreated toward the kegs. I made it a few paces when she called me out.

"Hey, weirdo!"

I turned around and Melody was smiling and opening her arms. She gave me a big, wasted hug. It was pretty early in the evening to be that sauced, but I was stoked she was in the party zone.

"I'm so glad you're here!" she said.

"Yeah, where've you been?" I asked. I should have gone with a more casual "What've you been up to?" but my concern leaped out.

"Just cruisin'," she said.

"You wanna get some brews?" I said, nodding to the keg line. I had to cop some of her vibe, or I'd blow it and have to fart my way out of it again.

"Shit, line's too long. I need to be drunker faster," I said.

"Hold on." She walked past the line of almost twenty people and went right to the front. She flirted with some guy who let her pour two beers. As she was walking back, unhazed by the crowd, I decided I would allow that flirt for the good of the beer.

Renaldo walked by us pushing a guitar cabinet.

"What up, dudes? How many times have you guys fucked tonight?"

"Dude," I said.

"A million," Melody answered.

It made me relieved and impressed that she could still handle being crudely creeped out and not miss a beat. I could tell Renaldo felt like I was ditching him. He was always talking about scoring chicks but spending time with them was illogical. Before meeting Melody, that would have made more sense to me.

On the outskirts of the crowd, I spotted a burly metalhead with his hands on his knees, puking intensely.

"Check it out, Code Green," I told Melody.

"Nice," Melody said.

"What's a Code Green?" Renaldo asked.

"Oh, it's a Castle thing," I said.

"Yeah?"

"Yeah, it's just this thing we do," I said, trying to move on.

"Whatever, dude. I'm gonna go Code Rock. If you're not too Code Choad, you should double down on coldies and get up front with the real motherfuckers."

"Cool," I said, not caring. I glanced back at Melody. The puking man was still going at it.

"Hey, TJ!" she yelled to the puker. "Can we hitch a ride back tonight?"

She definitely said "we." I hoped that meant something good later on.

TJ threw up the devil horns sign without veering his gaze from the dirt.

"You know that guy?" I asked.

"Yeah, he's cool."

"He's gonna drive us?"

"Beats walking, right?"

"Fuck, I dunno," I said, watching him stagger back and forth and now pissing. But whatever. Right now, I was a "we."

I ran into Rex, the guitarist of Tion from the Castle. He was walking around trying to sell demos out of a shoebox.

"When do you guys play?" I said.

"When the kegs run out, Wolfman."

"Why's that?"

"Cause if we play before that, only, like, ten people will be up front."

When they went on, it sounded like a giant boom box version of the demo. Their PA was weak and the vocals were all distorted. It somehow sounded more lo-fi than their tape. Half the crowd was in front of the band while the other half stuck by the empty kegs. Four songs in, they stopped and put their instruments down. Apparently the band only had four songs. The people up front wanted more, so they played the whole set over again as an encore. And then did the entire thing again. When they looked like they were gonna keep doing it, Melody and I took off.

TJ was thankfully nowhere in sight, so we were on foot. The road back had a bunch of vegetation on the side of it and we had to be careful not to get hit by cars. I played off being concerned about the traffic so I could hold Melody's hand. She didn't seem to care and bent down in front of some weird plant. It was kind of like a bush but with paper globes hanging from it. She ripped one off and stood up.

"Are you gonna eat that thing?" I said, grossed out that it wasn't bought from a store.

Melody peeled off the rough, papery layer and held up what was underneath to my face. A perfectly shiny, green, tomato-looking thing. She sank her teeth into it as I waited for something horrible to happen.

"What is it?" I asked, not hiding that I still thought road fruit was gross.

"Tomatillo. Salsa." She didn't offer me one or appear to even think it. She finished most of it and threw the rest over her shoulder. Large or small, it seemed like Melody took more chances in one day than I had in my entire life.

"What time is it?" I asked.

"It's ten p.m., do you know where your children are?" she said in a newscaster voice like the popular PSA.

"It's ten p.m., do you know where your weed is?" I said in my own newscaster voice.

"Right here," Melody said, tapping her pocket. I suggested we go to the tract of homes Renaldo and I tore up a few times.

When we arrived, Melody was mesmerized by the peaceful street. All the Porta Potties were upright and you couldn't see the smashed windows because the street lights hadn't been activated yet.

I tried to find an undemolished house, but I accidentally led her into one that Renaldo and I had been in. Renaldo had spray painted "fuck you" all over the place. And it bummed Melody out.

"You did this?" she asked.

"Oh, no. That's Renaldo."

"Did you smash this place up? That's pretty fucked up. Why would you do that?"

"It's totally Renaldo," I said, inching toward the door. I should have listened to him. He knew Melody wouldn't like what we'd been doing. I just wanted to play "house."

Melody walked around the first floor and pointed out a different piece of graffiti. "So, you didn't write 'Wolfman Rules' on here?"

Oops. I didn't know how to get out of this. She was clearly disturbed. It's like, no shit, I did it. But what good was gonna come from the truth? I wanted to sweep it under the rug and fuck on top of it.

"Oh shit, I don't even remember that. I was totally drunk."

"Usually that's a decent excuse but something like this is different... I didn't know you were this angry."

"I'm not, I swear, let's just get out of here." Maybe JJ Doobie was this angry. I couldn't blame it on him though.

"Yeah."

We walked back down the new street. I could see Melody looking at the other houses more closely. It was house after house of broken windows and she shook her head.

"What do you want to do?" I asked.

"Go to the Castle."

"Whoa, yeah! Can I come?"

"Yeah, if you promise not to smash it to pieces."

"Tsss, it's totally Renaldo, I swear." I had to keep throwing him under the bus and hope she would buy it. He wouldn't care anyways.

Getting in was easy. Melody had stolen a key from Jack. The whole place was pitch black, so we grabbed flashlights from the makeup room and walked around the Castle like it was ours. We went to the roof of the Castle to smoke.

We lit a joint and looked out in the direction of the ocean. A thick fog bank had rolled in that stopped just below our lookout. The moon lit up the top of the fog and it was like being above the clouds.

"I really like you," I said.

"Oh, now I'm downgraded to 'like' now that you're not super wasted," she said, laughing.

"No, no. I mean, like... you're different. Like me."

"How are you different?"

"You don't think I am?"

"I want to hear it from you."

"I don't know. You know other guys, like Colin and shit. They aren't into stuff the same way I am. I get really into shit."

"The Castle?"

"And you."

Melody smiled.

"I don't know," I continued. "Everyone's always just been like, 'you're weird,' and I kinda retreated into that more and more."

"Who gives a fuck what people think?"

"Yeah, no, totally."

I was supposed to have learned this already but whenever I started thinking about the past, it was like pressing the reset button on any lesson. I pretended what she was saying was a "no duh" but every time she said it, it hit me like a brand-new battle cry.

"I mean, you are weird, Donovan."

"Oh."

"Yeah," she said and got closer. "But you're not the only stranger in town."

That kicked off an intense makeout session. Just when it was starting to get hotter, Melody jumped up and ran off back into the Castle like I should chase her. I followed her flashlight beam with mine and caught up to her in the Throne of the Living Dead room. It had two thrones raised on a platform with zombified king and queen mannequins. We made out some more until I got the idea to jump up on the platform and sit on the throne like I was ready to be blown on it. I took the king off his seat, sat down, and had just claimed it as my own when the throne immediately collapsed and broke apart. It wasn't real, just some spray-painted Styrofoam with plastic jewels. I hit the ground with a thud. Melody's hysterical laughing made the pain a little better.

"You better put that back together before Jack sees it."

"Who gives a fuck what Jack thinks?" I said, trying out some of that earlier advice. I didn't believe it but wanted to see if she did. I also didn't think the throne could actually be put back together.

Melody shrugged and said, "Let's go to the storage room."

The storage room had all sorts of random props and scraps from old sets in it. Melody threw a portion of the Madhouse's padded walls down on the ground and we immediately screwed on it. The Madhouse walls were a much better platform for sex than the ocean. I lasted about four times longer than that first time but that wasn't saying much. Melody fell asleep before I did. I was too busy tripping out on how the better things went, the more I thought they could go wrong. Now I had something more to lose than just my virginity. I coached myself to sleep, telling myself to not break windows in new houses.

9

Jack assigned me to my first two-actor room, The Funeral Parlor. After the solitary confinement of the boo rooms, I looked forward to hanging with someone. A dude named Pete would be the undertaker and I'd be the zombie that pops out of a coffin. Pete was a pretty cool guy. He always had a lopsided, I've-got-a-secret grin on his face. He could have been a poker champion if he wanted to. His looks made him a born ladies' man. And his friendly-yet-detached attitude toward dudes made them admire his cool.

My zombie makeup was more complicated than a grease paint ghost face or a mask. I had to lay on the wounds and make sure it looked like bits of flesh were peeling off. It was a lot of shit to have on your face for ten hours.

I showed up to the room after Pete did and he looked like he was keeping an even bigger secret than usual.

"Dono, tonight's gonna be one of those nights and I need to know if you're cool," Pete said, taking his sweet time getting the words out.

"Hell, yeah, man. I got this zombie shit down."

"No, man. I'm not talking about this crap. I've got some friends coming through tonight and I need you to get my back."

"We'll scare the shit out of them."

"Fuck, man. I'm not talking about that. I'm going to slay chicks all night in that thing," he said, pointing at a large coffin, "and you take care of the room."

"Oh yeah, totally. Cool."

"You look confused, Dono."

"No, man. I got ya."

"Right."

"So you're gonna fuck chicks in the coffin? They're cool with that?"

"Cool all day, every day, man."

I thought it was creepy in a non-Castle way but yeah, whatever. Fourth of July had opened my eyes to this stuff already. The coffins were all super authentic looking—brass rails, plush lining, and polished oak. But they stank, probably from Pete rolling around in them all day, every day.

I climbed into a coffin. Pete leaned over before shutting the lid.

"Okay, so I'll do my thing when the plebes come and when you hear me say, 'He'll never bother me now!' and laugh, *'Ha ha ha,'* then you pop out."

"What's the plot before that?" I asked.

"I was in a partnership at a funeral parlor but I killed the other guy, you, for the full stake. So I embalmed you and put you on permanent display. Then you strike from the grave."

"But if I was embalmed, I wouldn't look like this kind of zombie," I said pointing to my rotting flesh.

"Who gives a shit?"

"And, technically, I'm not in a grave."

"Jesus fucking Christ, are you serious?"

"I just feel like this could be better."

"This isn't what it's about, man," Pete said with a look of "Don't fuck my night up."

"Okay, no. Let's try it out."

"We gotta get you laid, dude."

"I'm seeing that Melody chick."

"You sure she's seeing you?"

"What's that supposed to mean?"

"If there's any run-off tonight, I'll send it your way," Pete said and shut the coffin door on me.

It was a while before anyone came through. I was stuck in plush, pitch black and breathing shallow, hot breaths. I had never been in a coffin before, and had jumped at the opportunity, but now doubted my enthusiasm. It seemed more like some actual satanic hazing ritual.

We did the simple skit over and over. It was alright, I guess. Pete tossed me a couple beers he kept in a cooler behind one of the coffins to keep me "hydrated." After a while, it felt like I was just opening the coffin to grab another beer. Then he finally gave the secret knock on the coffin for me to take over. His chick had arrived and they disappeared when I came out. I didn't really know how I was supposed to work the room by myself. What's a zombie doing in a funeral home? I decided to just hide behind a coffin and do a simple pop-out scare. It got the job done enough to keep the plebes moving through. Pete finally emerged from his coffin with the sweaty chick. She kissed him and left.

"Good lookin' out, brother," he said and cracked a beer. I got back in the coffin and wasn't there two minutes before he did the secret knock again. I got back out and he was already gone.

I worked the room for about fifteen minutes when all of a sudden, a red-faced dad barreled through the room. I popped out to scare him but it didn't work. He grabbed my throat the second he saw me and nearly foamed at the mouth while yelling, "I've got two daughters and one of them just came out of the Castle looking deflowered, you dirty motherfucker!"

His choke hold made it almost impossible to squeeze out a reply but I tried.

"Not… me…"

"Try again. I got her to cough up who it was and she said the guy in the Funeral Parlor. And you're the only guy I see. How you gonna get out of that?"

I couldn't. The choke hold put me on the verge of passing out.

"That's what I thought, you scumbag!" He threw me across the room and I smashed into a coffin. The dad picked me up and just started wailing away on my zombie face. I had never been punched so hard and so many times in my life. And for nothing. The dad was out of breath but kept kicking my ass until I couldn't stand anymore. I collapsed on the ground.

Just then, Pete opened his coffin and another girl got out with him.

"Cindy!" the dad yelled. It was his other daughter. The dad instantly knew that he was beating up the wrong guy but didn't seem to care, and he lunged for Pete. Pete's reflexes were much quicker than mine and he took off running through the Castle with the dad behind him.

I was barely conscious, lying on the Funeral Parlor floor. The plebes passing by seemed to think my real blood was fake and all part of the show. And why would they blink at some zombie, curled up in a ball, crying for help in a place where that's already the norm? After a few minutes that felt like hours, Pete came back. He picked me up and a bunch of blood ran down my chin.

"Jesus Christ, man. I think you saved my life," he said.

Trying to talk hurt, so I didn't. I also didn't have anything to say. I was fucking pissed and didn't know where to start. He brought me to Jack's office where he had a first-aid kit set up and a bag of ice.

"Here you go, Dono," Jack said, handing me the bag. "Are you gonna be okay?"

"I think…"

"Well, I nailed that motherfucker good for ya," Jack said. "I dragged him out to the curb and told the cops he was wasted, causing a scene, so they took him to jail. Gonna be a funny wake-up for that dumb fuck."

The guys were being really chummy with me, and even though

my face and gut were hammered in, I dug that this was making me one of the boys.

Jack, Pete, and I just sat there going over everything that happened. I got to tell my version of the story and they paid attention to me like it was a warrior's epic saga. When I was done, Jack turned to Pete and scowled.

"Give me one reason why I shouldn't fire you for this, Pete."

"Hey! I pull my weight around here," he said.

"The only thing you're pulling are panties. I can't even believe you could get it on in there with that stench," Jack said.

"Oh, that's from all the pussy I've gotten."

"No, it's not," Jack said. "That's formaldehyde. What, you think I'd buy new coffins?"

Pete's eyes went way wider than mine. It was disturbing and disgusting news, but at least I didn't have my dick out in the things. Pete started to turn green and ran for the door.

"Hey, don't worry! I Lysoled the hell out of 'em!" Jack yelled as Pete took off.

Jack came around the other side of his desk and cracked open the first-aid kit.

"Shit, Dono, I can't tell which ones are real or not," he said while inspecting my beaten zombie face. "Hell, there are bruises under bruises. You're a tough guy, huh?" I wasn't but agreed. He cleaned me up and said, "You know, I wouldn't blame you if you didn't want to come back."

"Fuck that."

Jack pulled a liquor bottle from under his desk and poured two large glasses of whatever it was.

"I've got a question though," I said. "How do you even get a used coffin? I mean, like, seriously."

"Drink this down, buddy," Jack said as if he hadn't heard me. He handed me the glass and pounded his with a wink. It seemed like an answer. All this camaraderie I was gaining from getting my ass kicked made it feel like it was worth it.

I was too beaten up and buzzed to sneak in my window that night, so I had to do a face-to-face with Janice in the living room. I planned to play off the real bruises as makeup.

"My son, the drunk monster."

"I'm not drunk."

We were both drunk.

"You've gotten really good at looking terrible," she deadpanned.

"Yeah, it's makeup." I said.

She bought it at first, but when I sat down on the couch, I could tell she noticed. We watched a little TV and my nose began to bleed. She didn't call me out on it. She just went to the kitchen and came back with some paper towels and a bag of frozen peas.

"Here," she said.

I took the peas and we watched more TV in silence. The Castle Dunes commercial came on. I didn't need anything else stirring the pot and squirmed as the "Toccata" played.

"Just… Why, Donovan?" she said.

"I'm making money and I'm happy," I slurred. The shock from getting beaten up was wearing off and I was feeling the booze in its place.

"You sure look it."

Janice went into her room, turned out the lights, and started crying.

As the summer went on, cast members started to get bored with their acts. They'd get lazy and change their act in bizarre ways. Like, I know there was one girl who got busted for pretending to chew on a bloody tampon. It was ketchup. She did it for one day and got more complaints than anything all summer combined. Each cast member was weirder than the next but I thought the worst offense was from the clown.

I didn't think the whole clown thing was actual horror material. What the hell is a clown doing in a Castle anyways? A jester, yeah. But the clown's usual schtick was so boring and didn't fit in with the gothic nature of the place. He was a real loose cannon too, and now I'd have to deal with him.

Jack split up Pete and me after the Funeral Parlor thing and assigned me to the Haunted Jail. It was a double boo room. Two cast members would hide and pop out at different areas of the jail bars. One monster would set up the next, distracting the plebes while another swooped in, unexpected. I was back in my werewolf mask to cover up my black eyes, which I thought looked pretty cool through the mask. The soundtrack in the Jail was slow, hard-heeled footsteps walking down a hallway.

I staked out where I wanted to crouch when the clown walked in. He was a runty, white guy with a facial twitch and raspy voice. But today he was done up much differently than normal. In place of his traditional clown makeup was a fully racist blackface look, and he wore oversized baby clothes. After getting my ass kicked just yesterday, I wasn't looking to be around more trouble starters. And this was bound to ignite something bad.

"Dude, what?" I said. "You can't do that blackface shit, man. You're gonna get our asses kicked."

"Whhhhy?" he said in an evil clown voice.

"Dude, I'm serious. Why did you even do this?"

"Clowns, black people, and babies scare me," he said, sticking to the voice and tilting his head like a serial killer. I'd never seen the clown on break. He probably masturbated between the walls while hovering over rat traps. The idea of a clown in a jail wasn't even authentic. The Wolfman in jail makes so much more sense. Like I got brought in as a human and a full moon happened. The only way Blackface Clown Baby would be in jail is for a hate crime.

"Did Jack see this?" I asked.

"No, I have another master…" he said.

Before going further, I thought I should try to create some tiny bond with him so he wouldn't kill me.

"Want some gum, man?" I asked.

"What does evil want of candy?" he said.

It was going to be a long day. We started up and the room was working well. I'd set up the plebes by growling at them while trying to reach past the bars, and the clown would pop out with an evil "Hee hee!" at the end. The clown definitely got some weird looks, but no one said anything.

Until a black family came in. It was a dad with his son, about ten years old. As soon as I saw them, I wanted to say, "I am so sorry," but stuck to the werewolf thing.

"Grrrrr, let me out!" I said. The boy was scared and the dad smiled at me. Just as they were about to take their last step out of the jail, the fucking clown jumped out.

"Jigga-*boo*!" he yelled.

He scared the shit out of both of them but the dad changed his attitude in the blink of an eye.

"Oh, hell no. You're fuckin' dead." He lunged his arms between the bars, but the clown was just out of reach and laughing at him. The boy started to cry and wanted to leave.

"You think you can do that shit? You calling me what? Say it again!"

The clown kept laughing, making the dad more angry.

"I'ma wipe your face off with your ass, son!"

The clown danced around in a circle.

"Wolfman!" the dad called to me. "What color are you?"

I was silent. I just wanted to avoid getting my ass kicked. The good thing about the Haunted Jail was that the bars were real. We entered from behind the set, which made me relieved the dad couldn't get in.

"Oh, don't tell me, you some white dork. You're gonna stand here with this motherfucker and not kick his ass?"

"I'm really sorry," I muffled through my mask.

The clown kept laughing and said, "I'm not! Tee hee!"

"Daddy, I want to go," the boy cried.

"We're not going until Wolfman here punches this motherfucking piece-of-shit clown in the face."

"Man, I can't do that," I said.

"Oh, you some racist too, then," the dad said.

The clown did a little evil walk up to me.

"Doooo iiiiiit. Yeah, c'mon. Punnnnch meeee," he said.

"Fuck yeah, Wolfman," the dad yelled.

The clown kept doing the serial killer head tilt, saying, "C'mon, c'mon."

"Man, I'm sorry, he's fucking insane. But I'm not gonna punch him," I said.

"Wolfman, if you don't punch him in the fucking face right fucking now, I'm going to the parking lot and waiting all night for you to come out, and I'ma show you my baseball bat. You ready?"

"Yeah, dooooo iiiiit," the clown said.

The boy started cheering for me to hit the clown too.

How was I going to explain this to Jack when I'd get busted? I didn't want this to fuck me up at the Castle. Or start something with the clown that could equal being stalked and dismembered.

"I can't," I said. The clown relaxed his stance and let out a "Pfffft."

I looked over at the boy, whose sadness grew with every second I didn't lay the clown out. Then over to the dad who looked down at the boy. The clown laughed at me and that did it—I kicked him square in the balls, dropping him to his knees. The clown moaned as the dad and son cheered.

"Alright, Wolfman! Even better! You're not racist," he said before adding, "White dork," on his way out.

It mellowed the clown out for the rest of the day and he even acted a little scared of me. It was an easy shot, but I still felt like a badass doing it. And glad he wasn't gonna eat my face off later. I hoped.

When I got off that night, I saw the glow of Renaldo's joint on the beach. The closer I got to him, the louder I could hear his headphones. The music was unnaturally sludgy and warped sounding. He was listening to metal with dying batteries.

"Hey, dude!" I said, walking up.

"Oh. Hey." Renaldo didn't lift a smile.

"Sorry I've been all busy lately."

"Oh, yeah, me too, man. Me too," he said, taking a long hit.

"Shit has been getting so hairy in there," I said.

"Yeah? Wolfman needs a shave?" Renaldo asked, raising his eyebrow as he passed the joint. It was so tiny that it burned my fingers and I dropped it.

"Fumble, dude," Renaldo said and stared into the distance.

"Fuck. Dude, did I do something wrong, man? I'm sorry if I did. Shit has just been crazy, man."

"No, man."

"What's up then?"

"Did you ever just stop and think about shit?" he asked.

"Yeah, man. I feel like all I ever do is stop and think about shit. Sometimes I just stop."

Renaldo looked me in the eye and nodded. He was super baked but in the zone and present.

"I've been thinking," he said.

"Yeah?"

"And some of my thoughts are heavier than any band I've ever heard," Renaldo said, pointing at his Walkman.

"Like what?"

"I don't know, nothing…" It seemed like Renaldo was embarrassed. "Man, tell me, what's it like having a mom?"

"Shit, man. I don't know. What's it like having a dad?" I said.

"Yeah… I don't know."

I didn't like to think about the dad thing that much these days. In the past, I spent so much time screaming in my head about it that I had to put it to rest. As much as I could anyway. I had broken so many slats on my bed, jumping up and down on them, crying and pulling my hair out.

"Sometimes I think my dad was either the coolest guy in the world or just the worst," I said.

"That's what I was thinking too."

"Which one?"

"Both," he said.

"Yeah."

Both of our lives had holes in them that were easier to imagine than the people we actually knew.

"Do you think if everyone had just one parent, that people would miss having another?" Renaldo asked.

"Like, if no one ever knew about the two parents thing?"

"Yeah."

"I don't know. But I heard some lyrics once that said, 'You can't miss what you never had.'"

"Yeah, you can," he said.

I paused as Renaldo's heaviness sunk in. He was right, but I had worked for years to disagree.

Then we both spoke at the same time and said the same thing.

"Fuck it."

It honestly felt like the best and only way to lift the insurmountable weight.

"You need some new batteries, dude."

The next day, I became a full-time Satan worshipper.

Jack appointed me High Priest in the Church of Satan. The A-frame room was painted red and had goat heads lining the walls. I stood on the pulpit in a black robe and ad-libbed incantations from *The Grimoire of Castle Dunes* prop book. When plebes came through, I'd whip myself into a crazy preacher persona.

"Hail Satan! King of Hell!" My words boomed off the walls. "Let him who has understanding know the number of the beast! Six hundred and sixty-six!" I was in heaven, selling hell.

"Well, I just had to see for myself," a woman's voice said. I looked up from the *Grimoire* and confirmed what I already knew. Janice. The scariest person in the whole place. The horror of reality that I was running from.

Janice just stood there with her face clenched in disgust. She was trying to make me feel stupid. It was working but it didn't make me want to leave. I wanted her to leave. This was supposed to be my place away from that look. That's probably why she came. To show me that no matter how far down the rabbit hole I went, she could reach in and sideswipe me.

"Oh, hey," I said.

"So, is this worth it?" she asked, white-knuckling the purse strap over her shoulder.

"Jesus, come on."

"Now it's Jesus, huh?"

I stopped myself short of saying "gawd," when three screaming plebes ran into the room. I stood in silence, trying to decide if I wanted to embarrass myself further by doing what I loved. The plebes saw me acting more scared of Janice than the reverse. They could feel the tension and gave us both funny looks.

"Oh," Janice said to them. "Don't be afraid of him, he sleeps with a night-light."

The plebes erupted in laughter and ran off in search of better scares than a family on the brink.

What a low blow. I hadn't slept with a night-light out of necessity in forever. I simply kept it around because it was an awesome green skull. And also, if I was that scared, why would I want a green skull staring at me all night?

"This place is a giant toilet and you're pulling the handle," she said. It was hard to argue how accurate that had been for me a couple weeks ago. But I was sworn to defend the Castle and my cast member status.

"Why can't you see I'm happy here?" I said.

She gave me a head-to-toe look and squinted at my morbid makeup.

"Oh, you look so handsome, Donovan. And praising Satan? Bravo…"

My lip started to quiver as I held back tears and rage in equal amounts. The Castle was supposed to be my shield but I was powerless against her attack.

"Don't cry because of me. I wouldn't want you to start now," she said and dug a candy bar out of her purse, holding it out for me. Fuck. How did she know I was starving? I hesitated, reached down from the pulpit and grabbed it. But she didn't let go. Janice locked eyes with me and didn't say anything, but her look did. It said, "You may think you are the High Priest of the Church of Satan but you still need a melted candy bar from your mom, don't you?"

I wasn't going to turn it down. And I hated that.

"Thanks, I guess."

Janice gave me a new look that seemed to say she pitied us both and left. My sigh of relief was interrupted by the embarrassing realization that my co-workers in the next room would be popping out at her. I heard a monster bark and growl on the other side. Janice simply hissed, "Oh, just stop it already."

When Janice first told me about me working at the Roost and her keeping the paycheck, I thought she was being insane. But after seeing a Past Due notice on our door from the power company, I changed my mind. I had just gotten paid for two weeks and had a pocket full of cash, including a "You got your ass kicked" bonus from Jack. I wanted to spend it buying one of Renaldo's stolen bikes. It would make it a lot easier getting to work and I was tired of walking home drunk.

Janice always bought groceries on the same day every week, the day after she got paid on Saturday. It was Friday and the cupboard was in its usual dwindled state. Before I went to work, I decided to go to the grocery store and stock the house. Normal food stuff, but also what I believed to be thoughtful items like toilet paper, shampoo, and a *TV Guide*. And some shit just for me. I lugged the bags back to our house and put them on the kitchen table before leaving for the Castle.

On break at work, I met up with Renaldo and said I didn't have the money like I promised.

"How come?" he said.

I told him and he just gave me the bike for free.

When I came home that night, I expected things to be a little better with my act of maturity. Going into a grocery store and not coming out with just booze seemed like a big step. I opened the door and Janice jumped up from the couch in a fury. She had a box of condoms in her hand and a look of wide-eyed disgust. Shit, in my dash for work, I forgot to take them out.

"Whose are these, mister sex guy? Huh? Whose are these?" She was so pissed.

"What?" I didn't know what to say, I was shocked and confused at her level of anger. Even if I was doing something she thought wrong, I was clearly doing the responsible version of it.

"What?! This is what!" she said, shaking the condoms. "What are you *doing*?" Janice leaned on the last word with pure revulsion.

"Nothing." She genuinely wanted an answer. What was I supposed to say? "Mom, I slowly roll one of those over my raging boner and then put it in a dripping pussy until I fill the end up with jizz." This was going a lot differently than the condoms talk with Jack. My grocery gesture was ruined by my sexual responsibility. She forbade me from working at the Castle all over again. I pointed to the groceries and said, "But look!" It didn't matter. I had soiled its contents with my carnal lust.

"Nothing?!" she hissed. "Oh I know what nothing is! Where have you been *doing this*?!"

"Nowhere."

"I know where that is too! Dip Shit City, aka Trouble Town!"

My normal defense tactics of "what," "nothing" and "nowhere" were useless against her rage. I had to say something else.

"What am I supposed to do, not have sex?"

"No!"

"Where did I come from then?"

"That's my point!"

It was a bummer to hear that. Don't do this or you might end up with *you*! Jack's version was much better. At what point does a child having sex become acceptable to a parent? Never for Janice. She refused to accept the inevitable. She made it seem just as bad to even think about it. I thought she should be happy her son was exhibiting signs of normalcy. Janice always said I should "interact" with people more.

"This is so unrealistic," I said.

"I wish this was unrealistic. It's too fucking realistic! Everything!"

Yeah, it was too fucking realistic. The living room was too real. Janice's anger was too real. My failed stab at adulthood was too real. I needed to dive head-first into the deep end of Castle Dunes. And wrap myself in wolf skin.

I asked Jack if Melody and I could do a room together. I thought it was a foolproof plan to spend more time with her. He just said, "This is a horror house, not a motel."

"But we've got chemistry."

"This place is enough of a soap opera. You guys will just jerk each other off behind a coffin. No one wants to see the Wolfman's dick," he said with a laugh.

I was embarrassed and pretended to be professional.

"This job is really important to me. I wouldn't do anything to fuck it up. I just think if I'm locked up in some room for fourteen hours, I'd rather it be with her."

Jack sighed.

"Dono, Melody's a great girl but she's a free spirit. It wouldn't hurt to think that way yourself. It's summer, Dono." Jack paused. "Summer."

Since my plan wasn't happening I suggested to Melody that we dial in a different channel on the walkies. We used number six so we could crack jokes to each other. She thought it was brilliant and we kept them on for the full day. We used the walkies to arrange hookups in the Castle instead of taking our break. The best place to do it was still the storage room.

It was becoming one of my favorite places in the Castle for the obvious reason, but it also had all these fucked-up old Castle props. Like it was the designated graveyard for the place. I was usually up there before Melody and I'd rummage around.

The best thing it held was the old Dracula robot that used to be in front of the Castle for years. It did a few rotating quotes, like "Come! Come into my Castle! I vant your… ticket!" and "I bid you welcome, children of the night, to Castle Dunes!" I guess they had to take it down after it took a beating in a big storm. But now robot Dracula looked even scarier. It had a deteriorating face with dead eyes, exposed machinery, and tattered clothes. Robot Dracula was so much cooler than Colin Dracula.

It was still plugged into the wall. I shook it to see if anything would happen, but also just to touch the thing I had stared at for years.

Pow! It came to life with a painful-looking spasm and wriggled around. The jolt gave me an electric shock as it sparked to life. There weren't any sound effects hooked up, so it was silent and looked in pain with jerky limited movement. The mouth moved but no words came out. I put it out of its misery, unplugged it and propped him back up. The dead, red eyes staring through me started creeping me out. I buried him behind some old gargoyles. Sad to see an old friend in such bad shape.

On our sex breaks, Melody and I couldn't take our makeup off, so it became kind of strange when she would be doing Lizzy Borden and have some evil face thing going on. It was still pretty impossible to make her look ugly. There was also the plus side of the costumes. When she worked in a coffin scene she wore a nightie and I got to pretend like we were actually doing it in a bedroom setting, which still hadn't happened. I looked weird too if I wasn't doing a mask role where I could just take it off. I was a zombie once with elaborate rotting-face makeup on and Melody said she just wanted to do it from behind. I caught my reflection in one of the old mirrors and freaked myself out. In the middle of doing it, I started laughing and had to explain that it wasn't at her.

Sometimes there'd be awkward silence afterward. I thought things would be more relaxed. Maybe she was. I was too busy tripping out on anything my mind could get hold of.

"What's your favorite band?" I asked her. It was just shy of asking favorite color, but whatever.

"King," she said. The same band from the patch Renaldo gave me after I fell off the pier.

"Yeah, he rules." I didn't know anything about King other than that Renaldo was a big fan.

"They're playing in a week at the Arena Dome up north. We should go," she said.

"We" again. Knowing that I would have a week of us together leading up to the show felt like anything was possible after it. I didn't want to go back to being an "I."

By taking advantage of my job, I started feeling more comfortable about being one of the Castle gang. I was becoming like them. Partying, fucking, and abusing power, we were all under the same roof. The same spell.

I wanted to approach Jack about some suggestions. I had this idea for a new commercial. It'd have a big, fat Dracula and he's all, "I've been eating so much of your town, I've gotten huge!" It'd be a vampire's ultimate success—the wealth of obesity.

I went to Jack's office and opened the door without knocking. Jack was wildly pumping away at some young plebe chick, laid out on his desk.

"Goddamn it, knock!"

"Shit, sorry!" I yelled, slamming the door.

I stood frozen behind the door. Forgetting to knock was going to flush my dreams straight down. I was gonna be fired for sure. Who survives that encounter? I started thinking of fake emergency excuses to explain later.

Then Jack yelled from behind the door, still in the act, "Kid, let's go to lunch today. Meet me out front on the benches, I'm buying."

Jack sat on a bench in front of the Castle with a grocery bag. Parked on the curb in front of him was his Castle Dunes hearse.

"What should we get for lunch," I said.

Jack pulled two twenty-four-ounce, tall-boy beer cans out of the grocery bag.

"This," he said. Jack passed me one and cracked his open, gazing out at the passing cars. His gold chain was usually floating on top of his chest hair, but now it was tangled up with gross sweat.

We sat on the same bench where I got caught being a beggar by Janice. And now here I was, guzzling a beer in public with the owner of Castle Dunes. Cooling off in its shadow, I told Jack my idea for the commercial. He thought it was dumb. Said it wasn't sexy enough.

Jack didn't seem like he wanted to talk about the Castle. He was taking in everything around him except the looming five stories behind us. I tried to drum up something else.

"Your car rules. If I was rich, I'd buy it off you," I said.

"I wish you would! I hate that fuckin' thing."

"Whoa, why?"

"Why? Look at it, for chrissakes."

It had to be almost twenty years old. There was a good amount of sea spray–induced rust and corrosion. The "Follow me to Castle Dunes" writing had faded a lot and been sloppily fixed a few times. And the doors had been keyed up.

"Yeah, it's awesome," I said.

"It's good for business. And my taxes," Jack said and took a swig. "Creepy for most chicks though. For me too. It sure wasn't new when I got it."

A red Corvette sped past us.

"See that?" he said, pointing his drink at the car and spilling some. "That's what I want. That lucky fucker."

"But whatever, you've got the Castle," I said.

"It's no red 'vette, Dono. The 'vette'll get me laid up and down the block. One day, baby!"

"You can get laid at the Castle though," I said and took a sip.

"Sure, yeah. But the Castle is a few months. Its purpose is not the same," Jack said, wagging an extended finger off his beer grip. "The 'vette is year round. Not only does it get you from A to B like a motherfucker… but also! Also! With a 'vette… point B becomes Destination: Touchdown."

Jack crushed his can and cracked another brewski. He passed me a new one but I wasn't even half done with the first.

"You said the purpose of the Castle is not the same," I said.

"Yeah."

"What is it?"

"Money. Everything else," he took a long swig and came up for air, "is bullshit."

I couldn't believe that the creator of the coolest thing in the world would refer to it as bullshit. Or that it was just a cash register.

"So wait, are you, like, not into the horror stuff?" I asked.

"Not as much as I'm into Corvettes!" Jack said with a laugh.

I don't know what I expected him to say. But I wanted to hear about how our camaraderie was based on similar interests. Not profit motivated. I couldn't hide my disappointment.

"Hey, what happened, buddy? I thought we were having a great lunch here?" he said, raising a can.

"Nothing," I said and looked down at the ground. Jack kept

waiting for me to speak. I finally let out a tangential explosion. "I don't want to leave the Castle. I don't want to go back to school. I don't want to go home." I tried to add a more rebellious tone to it at the end, but I'm not sure it came off.

"Ah, come on, you don't want to be roaming dark hallways your whole life, scaring the shit out of idiots," Jack said.

It did sound stupid. Maybe if Janice said it, there'd be some good comeback. But it was depressing. I needed to enjoy the moment rather than stress its demise.

"Dono, you're a mack. Be a mack. Get into some trouble. Do something natural and super instead of the other way around."

There it was. He called me "mack." I thought it would feel different. But now that I was a mack, I didn't know how to act like one.

Jack threw his beer can in the open window of the hearse.

"Go for it," he said.

I threw mine and it smacked the side of the window and foamed up as it tumbled inside the car.

"What?! You weren't supposed to throw a full one!" Jack said and erupted in laughter. "Drink it up before you throw it away, mack."

At the next roll call, Jack came out of the back and Rebecca, aka the Countess, ran up to him. She whispered in his ear. Rebecca was a celebrity, known around Dunes as Dracula's sexy victim in the Castle commercial. She was a blonde super babe who looked like a prom queen five years past the crown. I never had anything to do with her because she was stuck up, and usually spent her break looking at herself in a compact mirror. Occasionally, she'd scoff at someone if they made a comment. But most of the time she kept herself busy being well groomed and on a pedestal. She was definitely the hottest chick in the Castle in the traditional sense, but she didn't have any of the uniqueness that Melody had.

Jack called out the day's assignments and said I was going to do the Maiden Slayer room. I'd be the druid that stabs a woman dressed in a white nightgown on an ivy-covered concrete slab. I don't know if the whisper to Jack had anything to do with it, but he announced that Rebecca was going to be the maiden. It wasn't her usual thing. Her normal role was Countess Bathory.

This was the first time I'd be working with a female "celebrity," so I was a little nervous but also excited to have some better scenery than usual. I think Melody noticed. She came up to me at the tables before I started and said, "No matter what Rebecca says, don't believe her." I thought that was weird but okay, I won't believe her. What was there to not believe?

I showed up in the room and Rebecca was already laid out on her back on the stone slab.

"Hey, there, that's a big knife you've got," she said with a wink.

If she wasn't so hot it would have been corny as hell. I laughed and mock stabbed her.

"I'm glad we could finally work together," she said.

"Yeah, it should be cool." She was coming on strong for a person who had never paid attention to me. But I enjoyed being hit on and thought as long as I didn't do anything, it would be harmless.

Rebecca pulled out a silver flask.

"Want a sip?"

"No, I'm cool. It's early."

"Oh, come on. You're no fun," she said, holding it out and pushing her chest together.

I couldn't refuse her delivery. I took a small sip and pretended like it was a bigger one.

"Yay!"

We went to work, and I thought it was going pretty well. Most of the male plebes who came through would perv out on Rebecca. They'd stare at her as I yelled an incantation to some four-syllable demon I'd made up. Then I'd stab her, she'd writhe around erotically, and the guys would hoot and holler.

"You're really good at this," she said in between plebes.

"Thanks, so are you."

"Let's take another shot," she said.

"Okay." I took the flask and had a nice pull on it. Getting a little buzzed at work helped make the time go much faster. That and staring at Rebecca.

A few hours and shots passed by, and I was getting drunk. I started slurring the incantation and Rebecca's writhing got even more sexual. Plebe traffic trickled down in the early evening and Rebecca started laying into me thick.

"You're really cute, you know that?" she said.

"Thanks, so are you," I said. My blood was running hot from her flask and the "Let's do something bad" look in her eye.

"Really?" she pretended to ask. "What's your favorite part about me?"

"Um, I don't know. It's all pretty awesome."

"Oh!" She pulled my druid robe down toward her and kissed me. It flowed right into a heavy makeout session. She pulled me on top of her, and I immediately forgot about anyone coming through. It was a completely different way of making out than what Melody and I did. She was greedy with her lips and more aggressive with her body. I got carried away and gave her all the tongue I had. My head was spinning with the booze and her hair pulling when, just then, Melody came into the room whistling a theme from a horror movie, dressed as an evil gypsy. She held a lantern and quickly dropped it.

Rebecca propped herself up and yelled at Melody, "That's for fucking Ronnie, slut!"

Melody stared at me in shock. I had been set up. The stone slab was a honey trap. Rebecca wanted nothing to do with me other than some revenge I didn't even know about.

"It's not what you think," I said. It was as much a cliché as it was a lie. What was to think about? I was dry humping the Castle prom queen.

Melody ran off and I caught her in the next room.

"Hey," I said, not knowing what to follow that up with. I grabbed her arm but she shook me loose.

"I never pretended to be anything I wasn't, but you did," she said and stormed away.

I chased after her but my robe tripped me up. I staggered and fell as she lost me behind the walls. I felt so dumb lying on the floor in my costume. I was supposed be a fake monster, not a real one. My corpse paint had smeared all over my face from making out. It sank into my pores and rotted me from the inside out. The stage fog buried me in smoke.

I went back to the Maiden Slayer room and shot daggers at the Countess, who was taking another sip.

"What the fuck?!"

"Hey, don't be mad. Have a drink," she said, holding out the flask again. I'd had enough.

"Who the fuck's Ronnie?"

"Tssh. Ask her. She's a fucking bitch. It's not like I made you hook up with me."

The rest of the day was awful. We still had to work together and my buzz was wearing off, making the remaining hours pass in slow motion. I changed my incantation to be based around punishment "for unlawful carnal knowledge," the acronym for "fuck." And I got way more pissed when delivering the fake blows.

"You're creepy," she said.

"I hate you," I told her. I went from humping to hate in a pretty short time. The Castle had gotten to me. I went on break.

I saw Melody at the end of the tables, flirting up some random druid with reckless abandon. She shot a look at me that said, "Stay away." I couldn't even defend myself. If I had the chance, I don't know what defense there was anyway.

10

"Dude, the Countess is a land clam. You need some metal," Renaldo said, passing me a joint under the pier.

I was bumming and didn't feel that the Tion demo would make anything better.

"I dunno, man. I lost what I needed."

"No no no. Fuck that. Dude, King. The fucking King is coming to the Arena Dome. You gotta see a metal show."

"That Tion show was kinda weird."

"Oh, fuck Tion, dude. I'm talking about King!"

"I thought you said Tion ruled?"

"They rule The Ditch but King rules the fucking world, man. I'll get us tickets."

"How much?"

"On me, dude. Least I can do to keep your sorry ass from crying. We'll meet tomorrow at the Arena Dome gate, like, at eight."

"What if Melody's there? We were supposed to go to that."

"Bro, metal is the great uniter. If you want to hook back up, then that's the place. But if you want to piss it all out, you can do that too. It's a no brainer, brah."

I had no idea what to do. When Melody turned her back on me, it felt like she took all of my bones with her. Maybe I knew what I was doing but I didn't know who I was. I went from semi-directionless to full-blown lost. But Renaldo's confidence and unwavering friendship led me to believe in his metal plan.

Renaldo went to the show way early to sell weed in the parking lot, so I hitchhiked later. I thumbed it for about ten minutes in front of the freeway on-ramp before a metalhead in his twenties who called himself Axe and his silent, permed girlfriend picked me up. His bumper was plastered in KRIF stickers that proclaimed it rocked. The radio station's promo spots featured a deep, monster truck rally–type of voice that bellowed, "*KRIFFFFF*, break the knob off!"

"Going to the King show?" I asked.

"Fuckin' fuck yeah, brother. Get in!"

His girlfriend made me jealous I wasn't with mine. Not that I still had one. If ever.

"Do not fucking hesitate, man. You know?" Axe nodded his head and turned it into a headbang.

"Yeah, totally," I said. Shouldn't there have been something before that message of his?

"I wouldn't be here if I did. You wouldn't be in my car," he said.

I didn't say anything as I began to worry that his stoned notions might be veiled threats.

"Let me tell you a story," he continued. "Sorry you have to hear this again, baby," he said, putting a hand on her thigh, "but fuck, it's so good! About a week ago, I was doing some drywall out on Sea Grave Road, you know? Some fuckers tore down about a month of my work, but whatever—I got hired again to do it all over, so I guess I shouldn't be pissed."

Oh shit. Sea Grave. I tried to keep my eyes from darting left to right.

"Anyways, I'm eating lunch and we're all listening to The Riff on the radio. They were doing that thing were they'd play one second of a song, and whoever called in and identified it right would get King tickets. So they got my ear, we're listening and they play the one second. I know what it is immediately, brother. It's fucking

King's 'Gypsy Dream.' Kinda rare B-side, I guess. I tell everyone, 'That's fucking "Gypsy Dream," where's the nearest pay phone?' All the guys are just like, 'Man, no, it's not.' So I'm like, 'Fuck you, guys, it's "Gypsy Dream."' But I thought maybe they're right. The DJ gets back on and goes 'No one's identified the song yet, here it is again.' I'm telling you—it's fucking 'Gypsy Dream.' You know that part where it's all 'Da na naaaa na naaaa da na naaaa na naaaaa?' It's the first 'Da na.'"

At Axe's request, his girlfriend opened up three beers and passed them around the car.

"So I lay back down," he said, taking a heavy drink. "Start eating my sandwich again, another song gets played on the radio, DJ comes back on. No one's named it. So I'm just like, fuck, man. This is bullshit. My boss tells everyone, 'Get back to work,' but I'm all, 'That song is "Gypsy Dream," and everyone can suck my dick.' I didn't really say that but I was like, 'Can I go use the phone real quick?' Boss says break's over. I go back to work, radio's still on. Man, ten minutes later, still no one's claimed it. So I had enough, man. I had enough fucking dipshits telling me what to do. I knew the answer and all these assholes were telling me to sit down. Well, I'm not wrong, you fucks. I tore my belt off, jumped in my car, and hauled ass to the nearest pay phone. Called 'em up and said, '"Gypsy fucking Dream," motherfucker!' Boom! 'You got it,' they said, 'Come get your tickets.' And I did. And here we are. And here we go! Believe in yourself, brother! Woooo!"

The dude was so wrapped up in his tale that we got lost on the way there and ended up late. When I met up with Renaldo he was pacing back and forth outside the gates.

"Hey, fucker! Over here!" he said and motioned me over to meet him crouched down behind a car.

It turns out Renaldo's version of "getting tickets" meant to make them on a copy machine.

"Dude, just help me make some perforations with this paper clip," he said.

"Is this gonna work? These tickets look super sketchy."

"It'll work. But we should go in separately. And if they call you out at the gate, just tell 'em a black guy in a red sweatshirt sold 'em to you for twenty bucks."

"Why a black guy?"

"Well, if you say Mexican, maybe they'll try to fuck with me—guy standing in the parking lot. And if I say Mexican, they'll look at me like, 'Why is this Mexican talking about how he bought them off a Mexican?' And if I say white guy, they just won't believe it."

"So why a red sweatshirt?"

"When your mom asks, 'What did you do tonight?' and you went out getting wasted and boning chicks, you don't say, 'I went to the movies.' No, you say, 'I went to see this but it was sold out and we had to see that instead and it sucked. We were totally bored and I choked on a Gobstopper.' See how it just sells itself? Details are what makes it real, man."

"Dude, I dunno."

"To the ticket taker, the black guy detail makes it like, 'Oh, of course he did.' The red sweatshirt detail makes it like, 'Yeah, yeah, that guy,' and the rip-off price makes them feel sorry for you. Now go before we miss King."

The ticket gate didn't have many people going through since everyone was already inside. I got nervous because it meant my ticket would be inspected that much more closely. I handed my ticket to a paunchy guy in his forties with a cop mustache.

He tore the stub off the ticket, but the paper ripped instead of a properly perforated tear.

"Where'd you get this?" he asked.

"A black guy in a red sweatshirt sold it to me for twenty bucks," I said.

His cop 'stache wiggled and he sighed.

"Go on in."

Holy shit, it totally worked. I walked over to the outside T-shirt booth and waited for Renaldo. After a couple minutes, I saw him approach the gates and the same ticket taker. He got stopped, started giving the story, but was then turned away. We hadn't factored in the ticket taker's own racism. What was I supposed to do? I was on the inside staring at Renaldo a hundred feet away, trying to decide if I should bail. He was waving his hands like, "Fuck it, dude. Let's split." But I couldn't. I walked inside. It was a cold-blooded ditch but I was powerless against the lure of the arena.

Renaldo's fake tickets were for shitty seats. I was way in the back of the place and all the way up top. I thought it was weird he didn't make rad fake tickets. I was perched among a patch of burnouts and people who came to the show to make out.

The lights went down and I didn't expect the rush that came with it. It was different than some touchdown cheer. Different than the Castle. Instead of scaring one person at a time, it was like scaring fifteen thousand plebes at once. A tubby DJ from KRIF came out to jeers and cheers from the crowd.

"This is Ragin' Rick from KRIF! Are we gonna break the knob off or what? I said, are we gonna break the knob off?! Ladies and gentlemen, *King*!"

The curtain dropped and revealed something more amazing than the Castle. Renaldo was right. But it wasn't really the music that made me stoked. It was the insane stage set. A mix of a futuristic city and Egypt, it took up the whole other end of the arena. A floor-to-ceiling pyramid dominated the back of the set, with ramps leading up its sides for the band members to run around on. The singer, King himself, came up from the ground inside a giant crystal ball that cracked open with smoke and lasers. There were twelve-foot-tall mummy robots that battled each other with magic explosions and more lasers. Lording over the drum riser, a massive, animatronic sphinx head split open to reveal an evil robot dinosaur that spit fire. Almost every song had its own theatrical element to it. The whole thing made me forget about ditching Renaldo and Melody ditching me. At least until the show ended, and I went to the parking lot.

There she was. Melody holding hands and hitchhiking with a girlfriend I had never seen. They were both wasted and yelling at cars to let them in. I kept my eyes on her and tried to stand around like I was doing something important. Renaldo was nowhere in sight.

"Piss Bucket!" It was Colin in his mobile bedroom Mustang, patrolling the parking lot, looking for fish in a barrel. He must have booked it up here after work just for that purpose because he always said metal was for losers.

I ignored him and went back to staring at Melody. I shouldn't have, because he followed my eyes and zeroed in on her and the other girl.

Colin flashed a wide-eyed, toothy smile at me and popped his polo shirt collar like it was his cape. He did a burnout and drove toward the girls. The burnout caught Melody's attention, and then she saw me staring at her. At the same time, Colin leaned across his front seat and opened the passenger-side door. Melody flared her eyes at me and jumped in the car, giggling with her friend. Colin stuck his middle finger out the window and did an even bigger burnout than before. I wanted to throw myself under it.

I was pissed and needed to blow off some steam, so I headed over to the new homes on Sea Grave Road. When I got there, I saw

Renaldo being put into a cop car. I didn't know if I should run away or try to help. What could I do? I'd ditched him once already and needed to face up.

"Hey!" I yelled to the cops while walking up to the scene.

"Take off, kid," one of the cops said.

"I called you guys to catch the guy smashing up the homes."

The cops looked at each other.

"Well, we finally caught the punk," the other cop said. "He's going away for a while."

"No. You've got the wrong dude. I just saw a black guy in a red sweatshirt running in the other direction with a sledgehammer, covered in drywall dust. Seen him around here before."

Renaldo's eyes lit up. "See?! I told you, I fucking told you!" he said at the cops. The two officers looked at each other wearily and nodded.

"Which way did he go?" one of them said.

"Down there," I said, pointing toward wherever.

"Can you provide a more detailed description?"

"Yeah. He was… uh, black, and uh, had, like, a red sweatshirt on."

"You told us that. Any other characteristics?"

"He was just really black." I felt bad subscribing to Renaldo's vague racism but it was clearly working. I would have felt worse if it didn't.

The cops uncuffed Renaldo without apology and took off in their cruiser.

"You're a fucking genius, man. You saved my ass! I owe you one," Renaldo said.

"You don't owe me, man. I'm a dick. I shouldn't have ditched you. You know, at the show and, like, you know."

"Man, I probably would have done the same thing. All of it. It's cool."

"Right on."

"But the show was sick, right?"

"Yeah, dude. The stage was awesome," I said while being reminded about Melody and Colin.

"Don't sound so stoked, bro."

"I think Colin is fucking Melody right now." That asshole. I couldn't hold back my depression over it. "And probably some other chick too."

"It's not time to be bummed, bro," Renaldo said. "It's time to get fucking revenge."

11

The next day at roll call, Colin really wanted me to know something because he would never seek me out to have a conversation. I felt like I already knew what it was.

"So, how about that Melody?" he said, nodding.

"What about her?"

"I guess she was down for the Count."

"Bullshit."

"Oh, yeah? I don't think that birthmark of hers is bullshit," he said. If Colin knew about the birthmark, then he had been there. The place I wanted to call my own.

I pulled Melody aside in the makeup room. She was rubbing some white on her neck, trying to cover a big hickey.

"You fucked Colin?"

"Kinda. So?"

"That's your response?"

"Who said I owe you one?"

Questions on top of questions were a bad way to start. I tried to turn it around but kept thinking of Colin sinking his teeth into her.

"Seriously?" It was the best I could come up with.

"Tell the Countess I said hi," she said and walked away.

I kept my walkie on our channel six at work, hoping for anything, a response to a sheepish "hey" or a bad joke. There was nothing but silence. Working as Wolfman that day became primal scream therapy. When a plebe would come through, I used to just go "Grrrr" or "Arrrggh" but now it was a full-on, raging *"Ahhhhrrrrrggggaaahhhhgrrrrrrr!"* I was really intense the whole day. The same way some of the old cast members and crazy people were. I buried myself in the role and let the Haunted Forest swallow me up.

Renaldo and I smoked a joint under the pier and talked about how we'd had enough of Colin's shit. I wanted revenge but I didn't want to get kicked out of the Castle or get Renaldo banned from the pier. I still needed this place. Its cracks were mine, painted or real.

"We've gotta figure out a way to get him back with no way for him to find out who did it," he suggested, taking a long draw off the joint and passing it to me.

"Yeah, but I don't know, man."

"Fuck this 'I don't know' shit. Get pissed, bro!"

"You think I'm not pissed? I'm so pissed, I'm breathing fire," I said, blowing a huge plume of smoke.

Renaldo's face brightened.

"Dude, I've got it."

"Yeah?"

"Oh, yeah. We spike his nachos."

"I don't get it."

"With acid."

"Oh shit. Man… how will we know the tab won't get lost in the cheese?"

"I have a whole sheet of bad acid at home. I tried one tab when I got 'em last year and woke up in jail, wearing those paper clothes they give you when the cops find you naked."

"What'd you do?"

"Uh, not important. What's important is that this shit will fuck him up. I'll put in, like, a few tabs so he'll be sure to scarf one or two at least."

"Will it kill him?"

"Nah, he'll just take the express elevator to hell for a while."

"How will we know it's working?"

"Oh, dude, we'll know. Let's do it on your next day off so we can go through as plebes and watch him melt."

Sounded like a great plan to me. Colin always had nachos and Renaldo was usually his go-to nacho bitch. I had never done acid—it seemed too scary, and the idea of bad acid seemed really scary.

I went back to work for the next few days and Colin proceeded to be an asshole as usual. It didn't faze me like it used to. His comeuppance was around the corner. Every petty thing he did was just another nail in the lysergic coffin Renaldo and I had waiting for him.

"What are you smiling about, Piss Bucket?" he said to me while eating nachos from another break table a few feet away. I wish I had known earlier that a sly grin was the best way to get under his skin.

"Nothing, man."

"You've got nothing to smile about."

"It's just a great day out."

Colin was clearly unsettled by my happiness.

"You're a fucking weirdo," he said, getting up from the table and whipping his cape around. He went back inside the Castle.

I called Renaldo up the ramp.

"Dude, he knows," I said.

"He doesn't know shit. It's on tomorrow. Don't puss out. We're fucking him back."

The next day Renaldo brought the sheet of acid and a hole puncher to the pier. We punched out little circles of the bad acid and Renaldo slipped them into his vest pocket.

"Okay, you should go hang at Circuit Circus and play video games until I come get you. Then we'll get Castle tickets and watch the show."

"How long does it take to work?"

"About an hour."

Dracula usually took his break around nine o'clock but Renaldo planted himself by the break tables for hours so he wouldn't miss it. I went to the arcade to kill time but I couldn't concentrate on anything. My stomach was in knots. I was too amped up and nervous. I wasn't really sure we should even be doing this. I'd put a quarter in a game, just stare at it, lose my three lives without a struggle, and put another quarter in. I thought about all the money I was wasting. At the beginning of the summer, I risked my life for this many quarters and now I mindlessly handed them over to the machine. I switched from video games to skee ball but didn't give a shit about all the tickets coming out at me, so I walked away. Some kid who had been watching me swooped in and grabbed them all and took off running. Good for him. I wandered around the arcade and looked for anything to fill the dragging time. None of the games were distracting enough to keep me from biting my nails. I sat down in a car simulator game and just watched the demo screen without playing. The high scores screen came up and the top three initials read DIK, FUK and VAG. Renaldo was clearly good at this one.

Renaldo finally showed up, wide-eyed and smiling.

"He scarfed the bait," he said.

The point of no return had been reached. I was excited to watch it unfold but a shred of guilt had crept in, spoiling the seeds of pending victory.

"Are you sure this won't really fuck him up?"

"Dude, what? That's the whole idea!"

"Yeah…"

"Get pissed, bro!"

"Yeah."

"It's gonna be great, there's no backing out now. All we have to do is sit back and watch the show. He's never gonna fuck with us again."

"Wait, wouldn't that mean he knew it was us?"

"Dude, stop thinking so much. Do you want to see him pay for all the fucked shit or not?"

"I do," And I did. He was right—Colin had to pay. We weren't beating him to the brink of death, we would just fuck with his head for a little while. I decided I'd rather be a part of psychological warfare than any other kind and ditched my worries.

We went and bought tickets to Dracula's meltdown. Renaldo had us wait in front of the Castle as he checked his watch every few minutes.

"Alright, it's time," he said and we lined up at the gates to go inside.

The druid working the door spotted me.

"Dono! How scary could this place be when you know what's behind every corner?" he said.

"I'm here to grab some ass, bro," I lied. But maybe I'd do that too. First thing's first though.

"Right on, doing tickets sucks. I never get laid. Slay someone for me."

"Yeah. Cool, man."

We shuffled in with a group of about twenty-five people and hung in the back. The thunder and strobe lights started up and Renaldo elbowed me.

"Get ready, dude."

The tape announced Dracula's arrival but when he was supposed to pop out of the portrait, nothing happened. We looked at each other and smiled. The crowd started jeering.

The portrait slowly opened with no one behind it. More plebes started heckling for Dracula. Finally, Colin poked his head through it like a timid groundhog. He looked terrified. People started outright booing him.

He crept out of the portrait onto the mantel and just stared at everyone. Kids in front yelled at him.

"Dracula sucks!"

It jarred some reality into him and Colin tried to do his schtick while being completely pie-eyed.

"Who dares…" he said, tilting his head quizzically at the crowd. The acid had him in a vice grip. He was under its crippling spell. Renaldo and I couldn't hold our laughter in. Colin scanned the crowd and locked eyes with me. Then with Renaldo. The acid must have given him a telepathic edge. I could see his psychedelic gears turning as his eyes rolled around like marbles.

"You!" he cried out.

"He knows!" I told Renaldo.

"Who cares? This is great!"

Colin looked like he was going to stage dive off the mantel but fell off instead. The whole crowd erupted in laughter. He staggered to his feet and started ripping his way through the crowd, throwing kids to the side in a wild rage. One of the plebes tripped him and he fell flat on his face, right in front of us. Renaldo was right, this was awesome. Colin tried to prop himself up and started screaming.

"You did this! You're all going to die!"

The crowd went from amusement to horror as his promise sounded convincing enough. Everyone ran out of the Castle through the entrance as Colin chased us as best he could, staggering through the vertigo and cartoon hell he was battling. The crowd was confused, but they knew this wasn't part of any act. We bolted down the entrance ramp as Colin swatted at things that didn't exist and screamed, "I'm going to kill you all!" The people lining up for the Castle had no idea what happened and laughed at him. Colin started throwing punches at kids but couldn't land any of them.

The fleeing crowd joined the rest of us on the sidewalk. Renaldo and I lost our breath from laughing so hard. We turned around and saw that Colin had picked up a small, long-haired kid by his shirt.

He stared into the kid's eyes as if he was a miniature Satan and began to lift the kid over his head. One of the kid's fatter friends tackled Colin and sent the long-haired kid crashing down on top of him. Colin was practically foaming at the mouth now and I began to see how bad this acid really was. He was totally unhinged.

Colin got back up and grabbed the fat kid that had knocked him down. All the pier patrons had gathered around and started taking pictures. Some knew there was something clearly wrong and others thought it was a performance to stir up more business. Colin wound up a huge punch, intended for the fat kid, as a camera flash went off. He missed the kid's face by a mile. By now, everyone knew this was as real as it was bad, and they started yelling for help. Some nearby cops swooped in and took Colin down with an immediate burst of force. This was supposed to be vigilante justice but now it was official.

Renaldo and I stood with our jaws open.

"We fucking did it!" Renaldo said, giving me a high five. My cheeks hurt from laughing so hard but I could also tell we'd gone too far.

The two cops held Colin down on his stomach and pulled his arms back while cuffing him. Writhing around with supernatural strength, Colin bucked one of the officers off, throwing him to the curb. The other cop nightsticked him in the head, and it seemed like Colin didn't even feel it. Some blood ran down his face and his Dracula makeup looked more horrifying than if it were expertly done. He locked his wild eyes with mine again and I saw what true madness looked like. I stopped laughing.

"I'm going to kill you! You're going to die!"

The cops didn't take to that and nightsticked him again, knocking him out.

"Lights out, motherfucker!" Renaldo cheered.

Everyone outside the pier had gathered in a circle around the scene and snapped more photos. They couldn't believe what they were watching. "That's the guy from the commercial," they said.

Another set of cops showed up and threw Colin in the back of their car. Jack ran outside and accosted the police officers.

"What the fuck is going on here?"

"Jack, your boy's gone insane. He was beating up kids and threatened to kill everyone. He's on something. Lord knows what."

Jack was baffled.

"This isn't something Colin would ever do, something's wrong," he told them.

"You got that right," they said. As they took Colin away, the cops told Jack to shut the Castle down for the night. Jack was crushed and dumbfounded. He spotted me.

"Dono, what the fuck happened?"

"I don't know," I said way too innocently. He could tell something was fishy and Renaldo's snickers weren't helping. Jack looked us over hard and threw his cigar down on the ground. He told the ticket booth to start giving refunds and stormed off.

"Let's get the fuck out of here, man," I said to Renaldo.

"Yeah, bro. Time to celebrate!"

We went to Castle Liquor. I bought a twelve pack and a bottle of Jägermeister. We retreated to the dunes, where Melody and I used to go, and sat on top of the tallest one. Renaldo cracked the Jäger open and took a huge slug.

"Jäger is the best chaser to revenge. That fucker will be lucky if he's even able to pick a strawberry after that," he said, passing it to me. Renaldo unburdened himself of all the insults he had taken. The revenge made perfect, justified sense to him.

I was torn. Part of my anger was quenched but it was replaced with a "what did I do?" type of paranoia. I thought I was good at mentally dismantling my enemies. I wouldn't fight but I could rip them a new one. Even if it was only in front of my bathroom mirror. But now I thought maybe that's where confrontation belongs.

"What's wrong, man?" Renaldo said. He seemed pissed he was the only one high on revenge.

"Dude… he looked insane. Like, gone."

"No shit, dude. Who gives a fuck? That guy made you drink his piss, humiliated you at every chance, and fucked Melody. Should we have thrown him a party?"

"No, you're right," I gulped the Jäger and cracked a beer. "Yeah, our punishment fit the crime," I told myself a few times, trying to make it sound right.

"Dude, this should be the greatest night of our lives and you're fucking sulking. He's gonna be fine, dude."

"Really?"

"Yeah, man."

I wasn't sure but agreed. Renaldo knew acid better than I did.

"I'm gonna kill yooou guuuuys!" Renaldo said, quoting Dracula. "Dude, that was classic."

I laughed. The Jäger was making me see the funny side of it. Even if it was the smaller side.

"When he ate shit off the mantel? Fuck!" I said, easing into my victory and buzz.

"It's a long way down when you're that high…"

"And fried!" I said, still attempting to loosen up. I was really trying to enjoy the moment but guilt kept gnawing its way from the back of my mind.

"Dude, you should be Dracula now. You'd kick ass. You'd get so much pussy, dude," Renaldo said, pissing off the dune.

I liked the sound of that and would be lying if I said I hadn't thought about it before. I leaned back into the sand.

"I vant to suck… your tits!" I said, laughing.

"Hahaha, see?"

"Yeah," I said. Then my thoughts froze. Did I dethrone evil to prop myself up in its place? Was it simple vengeance or a bigger, subconscious plan? Both? I always hoped he wouldn't show up one day and the cape would be mine.

I got up and brushed the sand off. Too bad my thoughts wouldn't brush off so easily. I hadn't considered the burden of guilt in our plan. I didn't want to answer the questions I was asking myself. The Jäger sloshed in my stomach as I swayed around. Then I got really dizzy. My mouth quickly started to water and I knew what was coming next. I puked a fountain of black all over the sand.

"I gotta go, dude," I said and staggered home, amused and horrified.

12

Jack held up the "Dunes Times" front page in front of everyone at roll call. It featured a picture of Colin with crazy eyes, swinging on a little kid. The boy looked terrified. The headline read, "A Castle in Ruin." It went on about how Colin was representative of the whole Castle and how it had become an unwanted scar across the face of Dunes.

"We are fucked," Jack said, throwing it on the table. "Someone tell me what happened." He was looking right at me. I stared right back, pretending to wait for an answer with everyone else.

"Dono, you were outside. What happened?"

"He just went nuts. Like he was on something."

The druid working the door that night backed me up.

"Yeah, he just ran out of the Castle, attacking people like crazy."

"Colin didn't do any drugs. That's one of the reasons why I could depend on him. Next answer."

"What happened to him?" I asked.

"He's gonna be fine. He's locked up but he'll be out tomorrow. They have to keep him there until he comes back to Earth."

I realized that when he did come back, he would pin it all on Renaldo and me. This is something I didn't think about before. But I also knew it'd be impossible to prove. That was the evil, semi-genius of the plan.

"What's gonna happen with the Castle?" Melody asked. She had positioned herself on the opposite side of the cast members, away from me.

"That's yet to be seen. But we all know the city hates us. The administration that approved this place is long gone. Probably because of us. I'm not gonna lie, I think we should tone it down from now on."

Everyone objected and groaned. Because we'd poisoned Dracula, the Castle was going to be watered down. I began to fill with regret. Even more than before.

"I don't want to hear it. It's your summer job but it's my ass. Just stick to cheesy shit and don't make anyone piss their pants until this blows over, if it even does."

I had gotten so wrapped up in the Castle that I hadn't even seen an end to the summer. Or that the ripple effect of bad acid would reach City Hall and dictate how our jobs would proceed. Or affect Jack's livelihood.

"We need a new Dracula," Jack said.

A bunch of guys raised their hands.

"Let's try out a few of you guys and see who works out the best," Jack said.

"What about Donovan?" Melody said. I couldn't believe it. I thought we were all fucked up but here she was, nominating me for the mantel. I looked over at her and she just shrugged like nothing happened between us. A few other cast members agreed, some of them I didn't even know.

"Maybe," Jack said, staring at me. He knew something was up. "Donovan, today you're on Electric Chair. We'll check out your Dracula tomorrow."

My Dracula. I didn't even know if I wanted that anymore. Something was up. And Electric Chair? That had to be a bad sign.

"TJ, get the cape on, you're in there today. I need you to seriously not fuck anyone back there, okay? We gotta wait for the"—Jack cleared his throat before continuing—"smoke to blow over, if it does. Then we can all act like jerks again."

Being in the Electric Chair room might be the worst job in the whole place. Worse than cleaning up rats and puke. You were seriously tied into the thing with leather straps across the wrists and legs. Like the coffins and Jack's hearse, the origin of the chair was probably real.

The job relied on the cast member working the room next door to come in and check on you frequently. But I was screwed—the clown was working next door. When he was tying me in, he kept grinning with his head tilted.

"Hey, dude. Are you still mad about the whole kicking thing?" I asked.

He tilted his head in the other direction and stuck to his intense, unblinking stare.

"So you're gonna, like, check in on me, right?"

He tilted his head again and left.

"Bro, I'll buy you a churro!" I pleaded as he disappeared. I could always ask a plebe to untie me, but they might think it was part of the act and just keep going. I got worried. The plebes started coming in and I repeated the same punishment over and over. Strobe lights flashed with a loud, electrical crackling sound and I'd convulse around and then die. The tape comes back around, sets me up again, and I'd do it all over. And over. This job, or punishment, was true torture. Because being tied down meant that if someone wanted to rush into the room and mess with you, they easily could. Pretty much anything bad that could happen, would happen.

First, a burly, football player–type came in, laughed at my bit, and slowly farted in my face. The smell just hung in the room since there wasn't any ventilation. Then a storm rolled in outside and got bigger and bigger with every hour. The wind and rain were so strong that the Castle started rocking back and forth. It wasn't like you couldn't walk across the room but it was enough to make you not want to be strapped into an Electric Chair. I knew the Castle wasn't made of stone but the storm exposed its cheapness more than ever. I kept yelling for the clown to save me. No response. The rain reduced the customers down to a trickle, but a few were still coming through. I pleaded with two teenage girls to untie me. They thought it was part of the act and giggled away. Eventually, three drunk dudes my age entered my room and I tried again.

"Dudes, I need you to untie me, I'm serious. I need to get out of here. I'm not joking."

"Whoa, he is tied down."

"Dude, I dare you to pour soda on his head," another told him.

"Fuck it, I'll do it," the third said and went right up and threw the Coke in my face. It was humiliating but also refreshing.

"You assholes, get me out of here!" I yelled.

The other two started throwing pennies at my face while they laughed.

I yelled for the clown as the boys got bored and left. The clown's revenge was painfully genius. I later found out that his room next door was empty all day. He just went home after he tied me down and let the Castle do the rest. I couldn't help but wonder if Jack had set this all up or if it was just a terrible coincidence. It was well past my break, but thankfully I didn't have to use the bathroom. I was sweating it all out in the prisoner's jumpsuit. The Castle kept rocking back and forth as the lights flickered.

And then I started to smell smoke. Not stage fog. Not pot. But smoke. It was faint at first but started getting stronger and more toxic smelling. Then I could actually see plumes of it creep into the room. Suddenly, a bunch of plebes and cast members ran past my room, all yelling "FIRE!"

I freaked and screamed at them to let me out. There was too much terror in their eyes for them to see me. They were gone as soon as they arrived. The electric chair sounds were going off and the strobe lights amplified the real horror of the situation. Flames began crawling up the walls of my room and spread quickly over the crappy decorations all around me.

Finally, a dad came through with his son in his arms.

"Untie me, I'm going to die for real!" I screamed. He unhooked a buckle on my wrist and ran out with his kid. I undid the rest and took off through the rooms, holding the neck of my jumpsuit over my face to avoid inhaling the smoke. It wasn't just wood burning, it was all the plastic and Styrofoam props that had lit up too. They melted into shapeless, toxic blobs. It looked like dripping blood on fire. The fumes burned my eyes and made me gag. All the audio tracks for the rooms and lights were still going, creating a surreal overlap of accidental and engineered terror. Stage fog mixed with smoke in some of the rooms, making it nearly impossible to see through. I was lucky that I could walk the Castle blindfolded by this point of the summer.

When I went through the Maze of Torment, I heard two kids coughing in a dead end. The place was going up fast but I couldn't leave someone behind like I almost had been. I found them by feeling around with my feet. I grabbed their shirts and started dragging them out of there. Now I couldn't hold my prison jumpsuit over my face, and had to inhale deep breaths of smoke while carrying their weight. I choked on it and gagged out a small bit of puke. I knew I had two more rooms to go and started to realize I might not make it with these kids. The Castle flames were making every inch feel like a mile but I finally made it to the long exit corridor. I was fighting for my life and coming to terms with my death. I could hear people yelling and the sound of the "Toccata" outside being melted into a slow, doomy drawl. Fire engine sounds swirled in the discord while people screamed for their lives. What were fake screams just an hour ago were now real ones coming from both plebes and cast members. I barely made it through the tunnel of smoke, and passed out as I heard Jack yell, "Dono!"

13

I woke up on a gurney in a burst of bright, fluorescent light. A hospital. The oxygen mask on my face let me know it wasn't a dream. My eyes burned and my lungs were scorched. Trying to take a deep breath felt like someone was sitting on my chest. I checked myself out and didn't see any major damage. No giant burns or missing limbs. The room held five other gurneys, all Castle people. They were a different story. Satan, my bro, was out cold next to me and hooked up to all kinds of tubes. He was wrapped almost entirely in gauze.

Suddenly, he started spasming and the machines made alarm noises. A doctor and nurse ran into the room, huddled around him, and started working with vital urgency. Then they slowly backed away. One of them said, "Eleven fifty-eight." He was gone. A dead devil.

Death wasn't rubber masks, greasepaint, and Styrofoam sets. It was here. White, antiseptic, and cold. The sound of death's presence wasn't the "Toccata" or taped thunder. Death was identified by a sustained flatline tone until someone turned the machine off. It was squeaky footsteps and the rolling wheels of a gurney. A clipboard being laid to rest. Death was no father figure.

A doctor came over. "You're gonna be okay," he told me. "You basically smoked a few cartons of cigarettes in a very short window. You're a lucky one," he said and went off tending to others.

The oxygen mask was freaking me out a little as the shock of everything started to creep in. I took it off and walked to the bathroom. I still had Castle face paint on and the stupid outfit. A few hours ago, I thought this was still my dream but now it was just horrifyingly sad. What's a member of the undead doing in a hospital? This was real life beyond the airbrushed grave.

I stared in the bathroom's Mirror of (Nearly Missed) Death. I washed my face with that pink soap that smells terrible. It took a couple rounds. At first it just smeared the greasepaint all around. I looked like the ghost of myself, the kind that would appear to you in a dream and warn you of Christmas Future. I pumped more soap into my hand and scrubbed hard with the brown paper towels. It wouldn't all come off without the Castle makeup remover. I looked old and tired, like I wouldn't need to fake-complain about work to buy beer at a liquor store. No one would card this face. Life without illusion was so much more sad and confrontational. At the beginning of the summer, I thought I knew who I was because I knew what I liked. Now I know the two have nothing to do with each other.

I wandered down the bright white hallway to the next room of gurneys. It was full of more Castle people. We had overtaken the place.

"Donovan!"

It was a familiar voice in an unfamiliar tone, full of sympathetic, grateful joy. I turned and saw Janice running down the hallway.

"Oh!" she said, sobbing and hugging me.

I had just seen someone die and I didn't cry. I let it all out now. Bawling. My chest shook with the weight of it all and we couldn't stop crying together.

"I'm sorry," I said and couldn't stop repeating it.

"It's okay. I'm sorry too," she said. We felt a connection beyond any other we had in my life. Far beyond the one time we couldn't stop laughing at the same joke on TV. I followed death for a summer and it was the real threat of it that brought us back together.

"I'm sorry for not, you know…" she said. "And I'm sorry the

pier burned down. I know how important the Castle was to you and your friends. I should have…"

I cut her off by hugging her again.

"Let's go," she said, putting her arm around me.

We started walking down the corridor—away from the blipping and beeping rooms and toward the exit. I could tell Janice was trying to think of more things to say.

"I know you don't like doing dishes. But if you want another job, I heard Ye Olde Times is looking for a busboy. You could probably climb the ladder and be king one day, the way you are."

"Yeah, I dunno."

We both knew it meant no.

On the way home, Janice told me about her parents and why they weren't a part of our life. It just all spilled out of her. She talked to me like a lifelong friend. I understood why she never spoke to me about it before. It made me feel grateful for my place on our shady family tree. We got home and I slept for two days straight.

14

When I finally awoke, I walked to the Castle to see its remains for myself. I needed the fresh air outside to help me cough stuff up and pick my black boogers. While passing City Hall, I saw Jack walking out, wearing a suit, with three other guys in suits patting him on the back. They all told Jack, "Congratulations!" with aggressive handshakes. Wearing a huge smile, Jack walked to his hearse parked on the street.

"What's with the suit?" I said.

"Dono! Thank God." Jack was beaming.

"Why are you so happy?" I knew it wasn't because I had survived, and it hurt.

"The city just agreed to rezone the Castle land for residential use!"

"Huh?"

"Condos! You're looking at the owner of Breezy Dunes Condoplex."

"Dude, condos? Why wouldn't you just rebuild the Castle?"

"Hey, I'm a businessman. And any smart one knows that sex sells. These condos are gonna be the hottest thing on the coastline. The city just bent over for me. Finally paid off, Dono."

"What about the people in the hospital?"

Jack paused.

"There's no answer for that question. That's my burden, not yours."

"How did the Castle burn?"

"It doesn't matter," he said.

He got in the hearse that was still dusted in Castle soot and rolled the window down.

"Summer's over, Dono," he said and drove away. I watched the hearse cruise down the street, until the dripping blood message of "Follow me to Castle Dunes!" turned into a blur.

The Castle was completely leveled, a giant black heap sitting on the sand. An oasis of ash. The only feature that remained was the iron gate, now tilted off-center by the fire. They had actually padlocked it with a chain as if there was still something to protect behind it.

Looking through the gates now, it was a clear view to ocean. All that was left of the pier were its salt-stained columns. A few people stared at the rubble and took pictures. All of them told memories of being there and ended their story with "I can't believe it." It was like a real funeral for a fake place.

One woman said, "I was there when it happened."

I eavesdropped for any insights but was quickly spotted by her.

"Hey, you're the electric chair guy! I saw you that night." She was impressed.

"No, it's not me," I said. She was confused, but I wasn't.

I walked away toward the beach. A car sped past and screeched to a halt. The passenger door opened and Melody got out.

"Donovan! You're okay!"

She ran up and gave me a big hug.

"Yeah, I guess. Where are you going?"

"Getting a ride home. Time to pretend to my parents that summer camp just got out."

"Oh, okay."

"So yeah, okay. Bye?"

Melody walked back toward the idling car as I watched her leave. Before she got in, Melody turned around and ran back to me. She pulled my shirt down to her level and laid a kiss on me like it was the first one, but it didn't feel the same.

The driver got out of the car. It was some dude I'd never seen—older and looked like a coke dealer.

"What the fuck!" he said, throwing up his arms.

"Hold on a minute!" she yelled.

Melody kissed me again and said, "Don't forget me." She went to leave but before she could make it to her ride, the car burned out and sped away.

"Fuck you, Ronnie!" she yelled down the road.

She came back to me with a "shit happens" grin on her face and asked, "So… you wanna hang out?"

"Nah." I never thought I'd say it. It just came out so easily.

"Oh," she said and got weird. I turned and walked away before it changed into something else. Whatever it was, I didn't need it anymore.

I walked out on the beach and saw Renaldo waist deep in the ocean with his vest and headphones on. The ocean was unusually calm as blackened pieces of the pier bobbed around him.

I yelled to him from the wet sand but his headphones were cranked up as usual. I took my shoes off and waded out to him.

"Hey, man."

"Donovan, fuck!"

"Yeah…"

"You're not a ghost, right?"

"Almost, man."

"Sucks, huh?"

"Yeah, I'll be okay."

"I mean the Castle."

"Oh, yeah."

"I'm just kidding, bro. But yeah, the Castle too."

"What are you listening to?" I asked.

"The ocean."

"Dude, you're in the ocean."

"This is way louder, bro," he said, motioning to the cassette player in his vest pocket.

"Let me check it out."

"Yeah, I made this tape."

Renaldo passed me the Walkman. The ocean sound was deafening and distorted through Renaldo's blown-out headphones. The tape of big waves breaking on the pier was strange to listen to while looking out at the perfectly calm sea. You could faintly hear the Castle's "Toccata" playing in the background. The now-extinct combination of sounds was frequently interrupted by Renaldo yelling at chicks, "Hey, ladies! What's up?" Waves and the "Toccata" were the only response. "Whatever, fuck you then." Waves continued to crash until Renaldo began speaking quietly to himself. "That's a sweet bird."

I took the headphones off. Renaldo had captured the soundtrack to my summer inferno.

"The other side is me going through the Castle," he said.

"Can you make me a copy of this?"

"It's yours, man."

"Thanks."

We stared at the ocean in different directions. Renaldo fixated on the debris floating by and I gazed at the horizon. Renaldo broke the silence.

"The Castle burning was probably the most metal thing I've ever seen," he said.

"Almost dying is the most metal thing I've ever done."

"Wanna get high?" Renaldo said, taking out a joint and lighting it up.

"Nah."

"Why not? It's not like you're working today," Renaldo said, laughing.

"I'm weird enough, dude."

"Fuckin' A," Renaldo said with the weight of understanding.

"Fuckin' A," I answered.

Another gap in the conversation came and I felt like Renaldo wanted to be alone.

"What are you gonna do now?" I asked.

"Now? Right now I'm taking a piss," Renaldo said, putting his hands on his hips.

It bummed me out to see Renaldo this way. I tried to think of a way to leave on a high note.

"Dude, next summer, let's start the band."

"Castle Dunes, that's the name." He didn't miss a beat.

"Fuck yeah, it's a killer name."

"We'll just write songs about the Castle. It'll be like a concept band. If it's not Castle-y, it's not us," he said while shaking his head in future disapproval.

"Yeah, man. Totally."

A souvenir button from the pier's gift shop floated by. I picked it up. It said, "I survived Castle Dunes!" I put it on, told Renaldo "Later," and walked to shore.

I never got a chance to jam the metal songs of the Castle Dunes band because I never saw Renaldo again. He disappeared in the same puff of pot smoke that he arrived in. Everything had. Renaldo, if you read this—call me, bro.

CPSIA information can be obtained at www.ICGtesting.com
Printed in the USA
BVOW08s1622160114

341909BV00003B/57/P